D1826313

Sputnik's Lore: Accepting Ourselves

Spiritual Lessons for a School Gate Committee!

Reverend Suzanne Winterton, D.Div. B.Ed.

© Copyright 2015 Suzanne Winterton

All Rights reserved

ISBN 978-1-326-31311-1

Sputnik's Lore: Accepting Ourselves

Spiritual Lessons for a School Gate Committee!

'What you don't know, is all I know'

Gary Barlow, *Dying Inside*, Sony/ATV 2013.

Also by Suzanne Winterton:

Life's Veiled Mystery, lulu.com, 2012.
Living Spirituality, lulu.com, 2012.
Lifting Life's Veil, lulu.com, 2012.
Chakras with Love, lulu.com, 2015.

To Rodney,
> who saw the potential,
> planted the seed,
> encouraged its growth,
> watched the blossoming
> and appreciated its fruition.
> "Onward and upward!"
> Faith rewarded.

Preface

"You know, we really must do this again; surely we can come together on a regular basis?" Gabby suggested. *"I have so many questions, there is so much more I want to know and learn, and I think that if I get a grip on what Vanessa has to teach I can be a better, even happier person."*

"I feel the same," said Frank, *"and I gather the way is clear for us to use this annex room whenever we like."*

"That's great, we are lucky to have such a comfortable place to meet, but we ought to have a meaningful name rather than 'the annex'. I was thinking about using the first letters of Spiritual Healing Energy Domain and calling it our SHED," she replied.

"Very clever," Colin responded, *"though our room is not very shed-like; don't we need something spectacular or adventurous like Enterprise or Endeavour?"*

"Um, those sound like names people would choose for a business centre, and that's not what we want, though since our explorations are beyond the earth, I was wondering about other space ideas, for example, 'Sputnik'; does anyone know what it means?" asked Frank.

"You mean the first satellite into space, launched by Russia in 1957?"

"Well remembered, Colin, yes."

"Well, our room is a kind of satellite, set apart from the school and village," mused Gabby.

"I was thinking about the literal translation of Sputnik; it means 'fellow traveller'. We are fellow travellers of earth trying to make sense of our journey and discovering wisdom of the ages

through Vanessa. No doubt we'll want our children to know about all this, and their children too. It will be our tradition, our lore - Sputnik's Lore!" Frank declared dramatically.

"That has an unusual and amazing ring to it," Colin commented, "it's just right! Sputnik's Lore: Spiritual Lessons for a school gate committee."

"School gate committee? What's that? I don't want to be on no committee," muttered Maria.

Malcolm called from the doorway where he had been standing unnoticed for some time: "It's like this, Maria; parents who linger after school are sometimes referred to as the school gate committee. They can be a teacher's dilemma, or a head-teacher's nightmare."

"I don't know about the first, but I'm definitely the head-teacher's nightmare."

They burst into laughter; Maria hadn't yet realised how amusing and clever she could be.

Chapter 1   If only everyone knew

Sophie nonchalantly rocked her baby's buggy to and fro as she waited by the school railings in the warm September sunshine; she ought to have been eagerly awaiting her son as he emerged from his first day back to school, but instead she was lost in anxious thought. Her day had been a mixture of tension and self-recrimination because her best friend had ignored her at the school gate that morning when together they had brought their sons for the beginning of a new term; both boys had raced off into the playground, normally allowing the two mums to chat and make plans to meet up for coffee, but this time Sophie had been ignored by Julie who pointedly became extraordinarily friendly with a new neighbour.

As parents gathered at the end of the school day, some idly chatted while others nervously watched the classroom door in anticipation of the reaction of their youngsters: Would they like their new teacher? Had they eaten their lunch? Lost their sweater? Scuffed their new shoes? And, most importantly, were they in possession of a new reading book, graded higher than the rest of the class?

Disregarding those around her, Sophie continued her preoccupied brooding, wondering what she had said or done to cause the stand-off with Julie. Throughout the day she had experienced the emotional extremes of anger and tears, compounded by misery that her feelings had ruined the beauty of a late summer's day. Obsessed with her thoughts, she felt outcast from the parental scrum; she ignored her son's excited greeting, grabbed his arm, tossed his school bag onto the buggy and scurried off towards home, angrily ignoring his pleas for her to walk slower and his demands to be allowed to play with his friend.

Meanwhile, Gabby was expectantly awaiting her granddaughter's emergence from class; it had been agreed that she would do the school run to allow her daughter to continue working. Their plan was feasible because it enabled her daughter to pursue a career and to enjoy financial stability, and it also offered Gabby a sense of purpose after the departure of her husband. However, despite this apparently ideal situation, the sophisticated grandmother became another self-absorbed figure waiting at the gate struggling with unsettled thoughts; during the early hours of the morning she had awoken sweating and uncomfortable, tossing and turning while her mind recalled her conversation with her daughter which had taken place the previous evening. They had been discussing how to create the best routine for the little girl as well as for themselves; their conversation had successfully helped them to share their hopes and confirm their plans, but hours later Gabby squirmed with anxiety as she recalled some of the comments she had made. Why had she said those things? What must her daughter have thought? How could she learn to express her views without sounding so judgmental?

Suddenly Gabby was shaken from her self-interrogation by a piercing shriek from one of the waiting mothers: Maria's son had emerged from his classroom like a bullet from a gun and was making off towards the traffic-filled road; her reaction was what the community had come to expect, for Maria was renowned for having little control over her children, and her youngest, now in the fold of the reception class, reacted just like his siblings; he hurtled away from his mother while she screamed her demands for him to "behave". Swiftly his teacher caught up with Stevie and firmly brought him back to his mother; undoubtedly his behaviour had been as challenging in class too.

While waiting for his children, Frank, a local fireman, observed the unfolding drama. Shift work allowed him to occasionally join the watchers and waiters at the school gate; he enjoyed the opportunity to chat with other parents and his presence created a masculine balance to the generally twittering mums at the gate. He rolled his eyes at Stevie's antics with growing concern that he was witnessing the early behaviour of another youngster who would likely cause the community services some challenges in the future. Briefly wondering whether the problem was the result of genes, the environment, or something else, he strolled over to Maria to chat while she attempted to control her wriggling son; she clung to the hood of the boy's jacket as he desperately squirmed to be free. She was grateful of Frank's pleasantries as she struggled to maintain control of herself and her child.

Meanwhile, a grey haired woman stood alone, somewhat aloof, surveying the after school activity; she appeared relieved to be greeted by an old man walking his dog. They exchanged comments about the weather and of the sad necessity that a school term had to begin on such a beautiful day. In some respects they were glad to be in retirement, able to enjoy the anticipated "Indian summer" free from worries about dates, deadlines and targets, but in the midst of middle and old age they sometimes wished for a turn back of time, a desire to re-live and to choose differently with a recurring thought: "If only I had known then what I know now…"

It was surprising how quickly the area became quiet and almost deserted as parents, carers and children were reunited and disappeared homeward. The elderly pair, having no children to steer and feed, lingered in the prevailing peace. As strangers they had arrived at the school gate from opposite directions: Vanessa had followed the path by a stream which marked the boundary between the village and fields where she searched for wild flowers, while Colin habitually walked a route through the village ensuring that he would meet as many people as possible as he exercised his dog.

Without a doggy companion, nor a child to collect, Colin wondered what had brought Vanessa to the school site.

"Actually," she confessed, "I'm a retired teacher, although not here yearning to be back in the classroom! I live nearby, play the piano and enjoy being a useful volunteer in school. I was hoping to catch sight of the head-teacher but found myself engrossed with the encounters at the gate."

"I used to be seen and noticed by the gate committee!" responded the old man. "I'm a retired teacher too – headmaster actually, though my stretch of freedom has been much longer than yours. In fact I would guess that I'm old enough to have taught you!"

"Funny how the phrase 'gate committee' has stuck over time," she mused, "you must have noticed how some parents arrive very early and linger long afterwards; their needs are more than just gossipy friendship, I think."

"I agree. That's why I used to be 'seen and noticed' thereabouts when I had my school; my aim was to learn more about the families and gain their confidence to chat about their everyday challenges – as well as listening to their complaints about my school."

"YOUR school! You are funny! So many head-teachers behave as though they own the school they run – then and now," she exclaimed. "It must have made it doubly difficult to have retired when your time came."

"Indeed."

Colin gazed into the distance and looked rather sad while Vanessa also became pensive. Sharing her thoughts she revealed:

"I can't help but feel their pain."

"Pain?"

"I mean their emotional pain, as well as their troubled thoughts. I find myself connected to hearts and minds when I'm around people. You know, so many of them experience similar struggles; if only they knew of each other's difficulties they wouldn't feel isolated or abnormal, if they could share their feelings they would feel more safe and less afraid. At times like this, when there is an atmosphere of incomprehensible fear, I feel the need to hide away."

"How awful for you, my dear; though I can't say that I completely understand, but I do empathise with any desire to help others find relief from suffering and grief. It's quite selfish really because I've found that when helping others, I actually find myself feeling better. Isn't there a saying: 'We teach what we need to learn'? After a lifetime of teaching, I ought to have learned a great deal! Maybe together you and I could be useful in our community."

The old man politely touched his cap, tugged at his dog and resumed his walk.

Chapter 2   Home Alone

Maria's presence at the school gate was pointless where Stevie was concerned, for as soon as mother and son were out of sight of the school he raced off kicking his jacket along the ground like a football. Indeed, Maria did not need to "mother" him for he was well used to caring for himself; when she left home to do her shift work each evening her older children found their own deviant ways of exploring life in the community, and Stevie discovered how to satisfy himself with junk food snacks as he lolled in front of his games screen. He was good at self-preservation and enjoyed life as he knew it.

Gabby's organisation around her family was quite different; she had carefully prepared a slow roast so that it was ready for herself and her granddaughter when they returned to her house. Her attention to detail for a nurturing home-coming demonstrated the perfection that had ruled her life; she was driven by an inner imperative to make everything around her neat, clean, and arranged in a particular way. Her clothes and possessions had to be immaculate, she took meticulous care of her appearance and she agonised over various healthy regimes for herself and her family. However, despite all her efforts to create an ideal lifestyle, Gabby didn't know how to be happy. Her phobic behaviour and irrational care of their home had driven her husband away, caused her daughter to be anxious and indecisive, and was now beginning to have its effect upon her granddaughter who waited with wary eyes for permission to play. The house was perfect in all material aspects, but it was never a home, and in it Gabby felt very alone.

Sophie's home had no sense of order; each room was scattered with books, toys and other possessions depending upon the family's particular need. She believed in freedom of expression for her son and his baby sister, as well as for herself and her husband. The house appeared to be messy, though there was an atmosphere of creativity and love throughout.

Sophie was grateful to have at last produced two healthy children, and though she wanted "the best" for them, her aim was for her family to be trouble free. However, her blossoming peaceful equilibrium had been shaken by the event at the school gate. She and Julie had been friends for some while; they had supported each other throughout the personal intimacies and experiences of early motherhood, and sharing the common joys and difficulties of raising a young family had brought them closer together. Now Sophie felt deeply troubled by her friend's seeming desertion and by the inexplicable change of behaviour; she searched her mind for reasons and for a future way to make things right between them.

Frank had no time for contemplation as he herded his four children away from school. Their house, situated on the outskirts of the village, was ideal for him and his wife to accommodate their noisy, adventurous tribe, and the comfortable home provided much room for exploration and self-expression for them all. The couple had been lucky to have established their home in an old farm; they had invested monies from their deceased parents and had produced a healthy brood, and so for them a family homestead seemed assured.

However, recent weeks had brought pain and anxiety to them both; Laura had noticed things were not right with her body. At first she wondered whether she was pregnant once more; her breasts and abdomen seemed tight, swollen and distended and her periods had ceased. As a nurse she wondered whether she might be experiencing an early onset of menopause in some dramatic way, and though she and Frank continued to enjoy intimacy and sex, she doubted she was pregnant. Together they anxiously awaited medical test results from the hospital.

Retired head teacher Colin had already experienced his share of bad news from hospitals; he had nursed his wife through the onset of dementia and with determination had continued to care for her by himself, but finally he had gratefully accepted the help of home nurses and carers who supported him until the time came for his wife to find ultimate peace.

Colin was good at continuing to care for himself and his dog, though there were days of loneliness when he couldn't help but wonder, "What's the point?"

Strangely the meeting at the school had caused him to feel a surge of well-being, a renewed interest in the day, a kind of excitement. He felt momentarily ashamed; surely he was not feeling some kind of romantic attachment to the grey haired woman who had been standing alone at the gate?

Chapter 3   Good Morning

The second morning of the new school term was definitely less tense than the day before; most children, now more relaxed, raced around waiting for the time to make their way inside the school building. The assembled group of adults fulfilled their twice daily ritual ensuring that their children arrived on time and departed safely, but Colin and his dog had no reason to be there, and his presence meant a rare early morning start for the long time retiree!

The old man was hesitant and self-conscious. He had responded to an inner urge to return to the school and, whilst pretending that his dog needed a morning walk, he felt ashamed of himself for waiting there without good reason. Nevertheless, he had spruced himself up in order to meet and greet his neighbours while nursing the hope that the other woman would also be there. He felt stupid, yet alive and excited; childlike, yet wise and eager; something interesting was about to happen, and knowing he was not acting with indiscretion he dismissed his fear in order to be part of the company.

Approaching the waiting head-teacher he called, "Good morning, Malcolm!   Feeling less tense than yesterday?"

"Well hello, Colin! Good to see you! Yes you're right, first day of term nerves get to us all… children, parents, teachers and of course, the head! After the long summer break these first few days seem more exhausting, especially when every routine has to be explained to the new children."

"I see young Stevie didn't get the whole message yesterday."

"Right again! Actually, I'm lingering to have a word with his Mother."

"Umm, I confess I'm lingering too. I was speaking with a woman here yesterday afternoon. She said she was hoping to see you... said she helps out sometimes... grey hair, about 60..."

"Oh, you mean Vanessa. Yes, she's a great help with music, storytelling and school worship. She's an ex teacher too....and... you're....looking for her!?"

Colin grinned. "I do feel rather sheepish, but there was something about her that made me feel, well, interested in life again!"

"Indeed! She's a very unusual woman; when you find her and talk with her you'll understand what I mean. Problem is finding her, and then persuading her to let you in to her mysterious way of being; but when you're on her wave length you'll be drawn deeper and deeper into ...well, I just can't describe...suffice to say she has been helping me a lot. Look, got to dash, there's Stevie over there about to create mayhem; I really must catch his Mum before she takes off."

Colin was left feeling mystified. He had never heard Malcolm talk of a "way of being" and "on a wave length" and what did he mean by the problem of finding this woman? Surely he could simply walk past her home in the hope of catching her outside or even find the courage to knock on her door?   For once he doubted the level-headedness of their head-teacher who had impressed him at interview years before when Colin had served as a school governor; then he had been glad that they had found a highly intelligent, compassionate family man who had imaginative ideas to sensitively improve their small school. What had happened to Malcolm recently to cause him to need help from this "unusual" woman?

The arrival of Frank's children ended his musings; the youngsters fussed over the dog until he jumped and yapped with joy making some parents smile while others clearly harboured thoughts that the school entrance was not the place for an old man and his pet.   Perhaps it was Colin's advanced age that caused him to become somewhat oblivious to those attitudes and potential dangers, and in addition, his usual clarity of mind was now disturbed by current deliberations; he wondered if Frank's renowned matter-of-fact approach to their community would help:

"Good Morning, Frank, so nice to have your enthusiastic children around at the beginning of the day. I wanted to ask how Laura is, but also, tell me, what do the youngsters think about the retired woman whom, I believe, helps out with music and things in school?"

"Who, Vanessa?"

"That's her name, yes, Vanessa."

Frank laughed.   "You've been missing something, Colin, if you haven't come across Vanessa!   She's quite a popular member of the school community too; most of the children are enthused about singing because she introduces them to modern music, she has a way of captivating the interest of even the older boys, and my youngest daughter told me that the children were so transfixed while listening to one of her stories that the lights went out because there was no movement detected in the school hall! Imagine the power of that! And by the way, Laura is receiving help from Vanessa too."

Colin liked to think he was at the centre of the community, but he was beginning to realise he lacked information about this "unusual, popular, powerful woman" whom, he thought, had briefly caused him to feel something special. It had been worth while making the effort of an early morning walk, even though "she" had not appeared at the school gate.

However, walking out earlier than usual meant there was now a long day ahead, and like a few others, Colin was reluctant to leave the gathering at the gate even though the children had long since been called into class. It was surreal how quiet the place had become; behind the open windows just a hum of educating voices could be heard, and outside a low conversational murmur and occasional stifled laughter from lingering adults broke the morning stillness. Colin's dog settled, sat and then lay down with a sigh; he seemed to know that the resumption of a walk was on hold while his owner noted the behaviour of the people around him. It had been a while since Colin had heard the chatter and laughter of women; listening to them made him feel lost and somewhat tired, and as he watched he noticed how often they smiled during conversation. Fleetingly he wondered why their expressions affected him, and then he became aware of two women who were definitely not smiling.

Sophie and Gabby had moved away from the group to sit together on the low wall at the edge of the playground. Sophie was clearly very distressed; her red eyes, wet hanky and hunched shoulders suggested she had been crying for a while, though Gabby was focussed upon the baby in her buggy. The child's wide eyed stare showed fear at the sight of her crying mother. Gabby had seen this expression in the eyes of her own daughter and knew the destructive power of a child's uncertainty around unhappy parents.

"My dear, what has happened? Are you ill? How may I help?" she crooned, not really knowing what she said, nor having any idea of how she might help the tearful stranger.

Before Sophie could explain they were interrupted by Maria who descended upon them like a fierce tornado: "It's him, i'n't it? That son of a --- headmaster. He's been upsettin' you too, I bet. Ought to keep his nose out of our business. How we look after our kids is up to us i'n't it? I'm gonna complain about him to the council, he shouldn't pick on my Stevie. First day at school and already he's got it in for 'im. What's up, love, does he hate your kid too? Once the council has it in for you, there's no 'ope, so maybe we could all get together and get 'im sacked."

Sophie and Gabby seemed stunned by the onslaught; neither knew how to respond, and both turned their attention to Sophie's now screaming toddler. The school gateway had become an arena of feminine pent up emotion. Gabby, now crying, watched helplessly as the remaining mothers dropped their heads and walked quickly away, but she was relieved as Frank approached.

"Now then, Maria," he soothed, "no-one is picking on Stevie. We all know he's a live wire and means no harm. Everyone wants him to enjoy being at school, and we can all help him to learn how to keep out of trouble, can't we?"

"Don't know how if he i'n't given a chance even on his first day," she wailed, throwing herself into Frank's arms and screaming louder than the frightened baby in their midst.

The outdoor hullaballoo wreaked havoc inside the school building; children strained out of their seats, and some sniggered at Stevie. Young as they were, they knew how to poke fun just enough to cause him to "lose it", and it amused them to see how adults reacted to unruly behaviour.

However, on this occasion the reaction of one particular adult shocked them all; head-teacher Malcolm stormed out of the building, waving his arms and red faced he stumbled towards the sobbing women:

"We can hear everything that's going on out here," he yelled. "Your noise is disturbing my classes, and having you linger here is not good for the reputation of my school. People will think there is reason for you to stand around complaining, and they'll think there is something wrong here if you remain outside crying."

Shaking and shouting, Malcolm had almost exhausted his anger as Colin reached his side; he placed his arm across the young man's shoulders and held on firmly in an effort to bring calm and sense. Frank remained in comforting hold of Maria while the other two distressed women turned their attention back to the crying baby. Colin and Frank exchanged wondering glances; both had professional experience of diffusing incidents, but this situation shocked and confused them.

Suddenly Sophie's baby stopped crying, Maria relaxed in Frank's arms and Malcolm's tension faded; the three pockets of disquiet became calm. In one moment they all turned and looked in the same direction towards Vanessa who appeared from around the corner; glowing from her invigorating walk in the morning sunshine, she made her way purposefully towards them. At the same time the school's administrator emerged from her office and expertly diffused the situation:

"Now everyone, I've put the kettle on. I'm sure there's room for you all inside, so come in and have a cup of tea. In fact, I'll bring a tray over to the old annex room where you won't be disturbed by the children."

The irony of her comment was not lost on Colin, he grinned at the assistant while studiously averting his gaze away from the other newcomer; he had deliberately set out that morning in the hope of meeting Vanessa, but having achieved his aim he found himself stupidly unable to greet her. He felt embarrassed and confused, but swiftly drew upon his recently perfected practice of hiding any emotion.

Malcolm was not able to find such control. He lurched towards Vanessa and almost fell against her; hesitating, he quickly recovered his composure and then reiterated the invitation for them all to join him inside.

As they made their way towards the school building the relieved Frank leaned forward to Vanessa with a welcoming hand shake.

The "old annex" was a room separate from the modern classrooms and the main school building. It had once been the school kitchen and dining area, but in recent years it had been mothballed and had become a place to store disused furniture and seasonal sports equipment. Despite its abandoned state, the room seemed comfortable and welcoming.

Frank and Colin dusted off a few chairs and placed them round a table. Colin's dog settled into a corner. Malcolm went off to collect the drinks tray while the ladies, settling themselves into a strained but friendly group, focussed their attention upon the baby.

Resuming his composure Colin inwardly congratulated himself on his decision to walk to school that morning, and upon the skilful way he had managed to stifle his emotional reaction to the sudden meeting. He was glad to have been able to help Malcolm settle from his moment of rage, and delighted that he was now able to have tea with the mysterious Vanessa. He pondered upon what he perceived to be the calming effect of her presence at the gate, though he was deeply troubled by the behaviour of Malcolm; what could possibly have caused the head-teacher to react in such an extreme manner? Why had he become so panicked about people's perceptions of the school? And why did he now seem so vulnerable when previously he had always been so very self-assured?

Chapter 4 Shelter

The annex room provided a refuge from the exterior emotional storm, and just like travellers who laugh and greet each other in instant companionship upon finding a communal shelter from torrential rain, so the three groups merged into one with a sense of friendly impartiality. By the time Malcolm reappeared laden with tea and biscuits their anger and tears had vanished, and as he handed them their drinks he seemed able to express their combined thought:

"Look, I'm really sorry; I don't know what came over me. I wouldn't want anyone to feel pushed away from the school; we're all part of a good community; please, feel free to enjoy the tea and perhaps talk and share for as long as you like. Of course I need to get back, but if any of you want to talk to me further I'll be glad to see you after school."

Despite his warm words Malcolm left the room looking rather dismayed, and whilst the group accepted his apology and busied themselves with their tea, Vanessa looked towards the closing door with an expression of compassionate concern.

Maria was happy to have been drawn into the parental group; on previous occasions, whenever she had dared to attend school gatherings, she had been ostracised by other mothers, but now in conversation with Gabby and Sophie she felt she belonged. The three women nodded and smiled as they noticed that the baby and the dog had both fallen asleep.

"Well, I think we should formally introduce ourselves," began Frank, "and though I guess you ladies already know Vanessa, I don't believe Colin has had the pleasure..."

Suddenly Colin's legs became weak; feeling nauseous and with a racing heartbeat he gazed in wordless stupor at Vanessa. The others exchanged quizzical glances as they waited for the extended silence to be broken, but Colin seemed unaware of the shared embarrassment and remained unable to collect himself or offer any meaningful greeting. His glazed expression lingered until Vanessa approached him and quietly murmured,

"It's ok, Colin. I quite understand. If I may, I'd like to just place my hand on your heart?"

Colin simply nodded and remained inert as he gazed at her. Thoughts floated around him: What is the expression in her eyes? What is she seeing in mine? Does she know my secrets? Why can't I speak? Why do I feel so lightheaded?

Vanessa's touch was slight upon his chest. His body felt hollow, his heart light, lighter than he had felt for years, especially since his wife had become ill; he felt her presence, and in his mind he heard her voice for the first time since she had died. He recollected how part of his ongoing torment had been that he couldn't recall the sound of her voice. Now she was clear to him, clear and strong, so different from her feebleness at death. He felt glorious, peaceful and joyful, and instantly understood the meaning of bliss.

Distantly he heard Vanessa's voice, "You're alright, Colin; just breathe deeply for me, though isn't it strange how everyone is watching us?"

With coughs of embarrassment, Frank and the women started to reorganise the tea tray and pretended to become very interested in other parts of the room. Frank had an inkling of what was taking place; he had seen the same glorious, vacant expression on his wife's face when she had tried to explain how it felt to have a healing session with Vanessa.

After a further few moments Vanessa indicated that she and Colin were ready to resume normal conversation; she thirstily drank her bottled water while Colin briefly excused himself, and in his absence Maria asked the question that the rest dare not:

"What the 'ell was that all about?"

"Hardly hell, Maria," Frank smiled. "More like heaven by the look on Colin's face."

"Is he in love, or sumthin'?"

"That's a wonderful explanation," Vanessa laughed. "Love is what it is, but, no, even though Colin has some fears about his emotion, he is definitely not in love with me! He has just been reminded of the wondrous love and trust he shared, and still shares, with his wife whom, I think, passed away some years ago."

Colin crept back to sit opposite Vanessa as she continued, "You see, Colin has been experiencing grief, intense grief, for such a long time. He thought he had got over the death of his wife, and indeed to a great extent he has. However, like many men, and some women and children, Colin has never really wept about her passing, his loneliness, his lack of purpose, his fear of life, and his confusion about death. Over the years he has done well to hold himself together by taking walks with his dog, caring for himself and his home, and by his sustained friendship with neighbours. But beneath all that activity he has been frightened to express his emotions and unwilling to just 'be' in case he 'lost it,' as the saying goes."

"You're exactly right, my dear," murmured Colin, "but how did you know these things about me? And what just happened between us?"

"I know because I know, and I can't help but know," she responded rather mysteriously. "Yesterday, I told you, I can't help but feel the emotional pain of others. It's a psychic gift which sometimes seems a curse, but during situations like this it is an absolute joy and privilege."

"So what happened?" asked Frank. "What did you do with Colin? What are you doing that helps my wife so much? And what may you do for all of us?"

"Those are big questions which I would be delighted to answer and discuss, but I am wondering if this is the appropriate time and place, especially since we have gate crashed – pun intended after our earlier interactions! – onto school property. We should take time to reflect, and for those who want to hear more, we should plan to meet at a later date somewhere in the village," replied Vanessa.

"Wisely said," responded Frank, "but, you know, this room feels so comfortable and welcoming even though it is only an under-used storeroom. If it were possible it could become an ideal neutral place to meet, rather than having to choose someone's home."

"Yes, and since we have a village without a community centre, perhaps we should investigate the possibility of creating a comfortable place to meet," said Colin. "Leave this to me to explore through the official channels," he added, with a gleam of excitement in his eyes.

"Don't see why we need official channels now we're just friends," muttered Maria.

"Indeed, after what we have experienced together today, we *are* friends not *just* friends," responded Frank, "but let's have Colin make this official; we ought to be certain of all the issues of health and safety, as well as finance, if this is going to take off," he grinned.

As they prepared to leave, they busied with an exchange of contact details, then Frank and Vanessa walked together towards the river path, Colin grasped his dog's lead with renewed vigour and made his way towards the school building, and Sophie and Gabby stayed to clear the cups, leaving Maria to explore the disused kitchen area.

"Say, you two," she called, "all the dinnertime stuff is 'ere, just like we left it ages ago."

"What do you mean, Maria?"

"I used to work 'ere;" she explained proudly, "my first job was in this kitchen, 'elping to do school dinners. Well, I peeled potatoes and washed up, but it was a damn good job till they closed it all. But look, all the pots and pans are still 'ere. If we really could 'ave this as a meeting place we could make tea instead of getting those cups from the school. Or even make soup or sumthin'."

"Um, a soup and juice club," Gabby mused.

"Oh, you mean one of them fancy fruit juicers?"

"Absolutely, we could have meals and chats that keep us healthy," laughed Sophie; the prospect of her day had definitely improved now that her mind was occupied with something other than her fear of Julie.

Like women preoccupied with future home improvement they made parting glances around the room before strolling to the main school building to return the tea tray, but as they passed Malcolm's office they heard his raised voice for the second time that morning:

"Ok, ok, Colin, I know exactly what you've come to talk about. I said I'm sorry, are you going to take this further?"

"No, no you don't know what I've come to say," murmured Colin. "Just give me a moment, if you have one, to sit and listen to an idea I have. Don't worry about what happened earlier. You're stressed, that's all. Everyone gets a bit anxious at the start of the school year. Chill. Isn't that what young people say?"

"Yes, yes, stress, that's what it is." Malcolm seemed to drift into a troubled daze.

"So, do you have a moment?" Colin continued. "It's about the annex room; do you have any immediate plans for its use? It's just that this morning's opportunity to meet there was wonderful, really wonderful. And I was thinking, well, some of us were thinking, that it would be an ideal place in which to create a proper meeting environment, an official room for the entire village. Do you think we could approach the governors and the authority? We would follow all health and safety regulations, and it wouldn't be a drain on the school budget because I would like to put some of my personal funds into the venture. We could…"

"Stop, stop, you're crowding me with enthusiasm. What's happened to you to create so much excitement?"

"What's happened? That is a question I want answered, to be sure. And if I am thinking correctly, I will find out by creating a meeting place to talk with your volunteer school helper, Vanessa."

Malcolm looked momentarily peaceful. "She is remarkable, isn't she? Whenever she's in school, whatever she's doing – singing, reading, group work – the place seems, well, umm, happy. I certainly approve of the annex room being of greater use to our school and the wider community, but, you know, you've already donated a lot of money… In fact I'm looking forward to my pension if it's as plentiful as yours! Yes! Let me pursue your idea, and in the meantime I'll send out a group invitation for meetings to take place in there rather than at the gate. You know how school gate committees can be alarming – other parents really will think there is something wrong here."

Colin couldn't help but notice the reappearance of concern in Malcolm's eyes, like a scared rabbit, he thought. But he was delighted with the head teacher's response to his community idea, and as he walked home he chatted excitedly to his dog.

Meanwhile, as he accompanied Vanessa towards her home, Frank tried to express his gratitude for the attention she was giving to his wife during what they believed to be an impending health crisis. Uncharacteristically he found his speech hesitant as he choked back tears. Normally articulate, courageous and consistently strong as the leader of the local fire fighters, he was unnerved to find himself lost for words with tears rolling down his cheeks.

"Sorry, sorry," he cried, "I, I …"

Standing by a freshly harvested field, where a skylark sang high in the expanse of the deep blue sky, they breathed in the sun-soaked air and Vanessa placed her hand firmly in the centre of Frank's back allowing and encouraging him to sob profusely. After a few minutes his heaving body stilled and his tears ceased; he looked towards her and smiled. Gazing into her dark eyes, he searched their depths and pondered the sentiment behind her expression; then he recollected Maria's words: "Is it love or something?"

"There," she said, "all is well now."

Chapter 5   Major Decision

Gabby, Sophie and Maria had no need to set aside dates for their meetings since they were committed to the twice daily school run, and having received Malcolm's invitation they habitually made their way to the annex room where they were pleased to chat and quite glad to avoid him; instinctively they kept quiet about the head-teacher's two emotional outbursts, but in the safety of the room they felt able to talk freely.   They eagerly anticipated a forthcoming opportunity for the group's gathering, but knew that it was dependent upon Frank's work shifts; he had shared his schedule with them and with Colin, but they wondered how Vanessa would be kept "in the loop."

"Oh, she'll know when to arrive," Frank assured them in a rather mysterious tone.   "I'm so looking forward to our next meeting, and I trust it will be one of many.   I hope you don't mind, I've talked about the group with my wife and suggested that she should join us."

"We'll be glad to meet her," said Gabby, "and we think it would be good to have Malcolm there too, but since the gathering is likely to be during the day he will be unable to come.   You know, we really need him to be there, or should I say, he really needs to be there?"

"I understand what you are saying," said Frank, cautiously, "and I wonder how that can be managed; perhaps over time we will have evening meetings as well as daytime ones?   I've heard Colin has some big ideas for this venture, though maybe we're getting carried away with possibilities even before our first scheduled get-together?"

"Well, Sophie, Maria and I are already on a roll! During your shift work we've been creatively busy in the meeting room, and you will not be surprised to hear that whenever we are there it's not long before Colin and his dog turn up!"

Sophie's husband had noted a substantial improvement in his wife's demeanour as a result of her being occupied with the village group. After the emotional drama at the beginning of the new school year he had worried about the reappearance of her quiet crying episodes and her uncharacteristic short temper with their children; as always she had shared what had taken place between her and Julie, and he too had been unable to comprehend their difficulty. His problem was exacerbated by the continued close friendship between himself and Julie's husband. Indeed, throughout their early marriages and the subsequent arrival of babies they had been a close foursome, but now he felt unable to discuss the fracas with his friend, and so their relationship continued without either of them speaking of the rift between their wives. What could possibly have happened between the women? How could it be understood and mended?

In the meantime he was glad to feel Sophie's growing contentment, relieved that their children were beginning to be less fractious around their mother, and hoped that one day her smiling, fun-loving nature would fully return so that they could enjoy each other again as they had during the early days of their marriage. Their current lack of intimacy troubled him. Was it her? Or himself? Had their difficulties arisen because of tiredness at home and work? Was it stress? Money concerns? Had they become overwhelmed by fear due to their increased responsibility as maturing parents? Or were they simply falling out of love? He had no idea how to address their difficulty and was not in the habit of sharing with anyone other than Sophie, yet paradoxically, she was not the one with whom he thought he could discuss his escalating anxieties. She had come through a depressive illness after losing their first two children, so he definitely didn't want to unsettle their relationship now that she seemed to be rediscovering her peace of mind. He was happy to listen as she chatted about her new friend Gabby, and glad to learn how they were working with others to create something meaningful in the community, but he was wary when Sophie talked about the woman called Vanessa; the accounts of her activities sounded rather strange, and he thought she was probably someone whom he ought to avoid.

Gabby had decided that she should avoid talking to her daughter about her activity at school because she was unsure what the reaction might be. Her mind laboured over a variety of considerations: Was she becoming involved in out of school meetings which ought to be for parents only? Would her daughter think she was inappropriately taking her place? And would her interference mean that her daughter might be left out of parental commitments?

Eventually she convinced herself that the meetings were not connected to school, but then she wondered what exactly they were about. In her mind she repeated the same anxious questions: What had she become involved in? And why did it feel so fulfilling?

She knew she could not talk with her estranged husband; had he been available he would not have shown any interest in what she had to say; in fact, he had never tried to understand her and had consistently called her stupid, ignorant and useless; he treated her just as her father had done throughout her childhood and adolescence. She recalled reading about a psychological situation where some women are attracted to men with similar personalities to their father; subsequently, they marry and find themselves continuing to be oppressed by the same emotional burden. She thought she would ask Vanessa about it during their meeting…

Maria had not thought much about the developing friendships; she was not in the habit of thinking or talking about anything. For her and her husband, everyday existence focussed upon earning enough money to pay the rent and feed their large family. Life was simple: go to work, work hard, get wages, spend hard and make sure the kids are made to do the same. Her house was as clean as she could make it, and she loved her family in a way that she understood love, but in achieving these things there was no time and no need for emotional expression or deliberation about life. She and her husband had nothing to talk about because they had no idea that anything needed to be said.

However, the school gate encounter had tweaked something unfamiliar inside her; while at work she smiled to herself, and during a shift break she took notice of her reflection in a mirror: she paused, raised her head slightly to one side, adjusted her collar and patted her hair; she felt an unusual sense of inner warmth because, although she hadn't yet realised, for the first time in her life she was bathed in self-esteem.

Colin was keenly aware of the emergence of a new attitude when he was at home; he had not changed his routine since his encounter with Vanessa, but now, inexplicably, he did not feel lonely - now he was sure he was not alone. He looked forward to discovering how the solid, cold grief he had known for years had melted into warm hearted self-contentment.

He soon learned that his lessons in spirituality were about to begin, when late into the evening he was disturbed by the sound of his front doorbell, persistent knocking and shouts through the letter box:

"Colin, it's me, Malcolm. Don't worry, there's nothing wrong, I just want to speak with you."

"Now? It's late. Are you sure you're all right?" Colin welcomed Malcolm into his living room. "The last time you visited me at this hour was when…well, never mind when it was. That time is long gone, and I'm feeling much better now thanks to you and your Vanessa."

"She's not my Vanessa, but it is her I want to talk to you about. Just now, as I was leaving school, I made a decision about your proposed gathering in the annex room. I was thinking, the group will have to meet during the day, which ought to leave me out, but I have decided to create time for myself to join you. There are important reasons for me to be there. You're aware that I regularly set aside time for all my staff for their professional development, and I ought to do the same for myself. I will do my office work late into the evenings which will release a short time during my working day to attend the group meeting with Vanessa. I have spoken to her about this and she will be delighted to meet with us whenever we can liaise with Frank's work shifts. What do you think?" He finished, breathlessly.

"I am highly delighted, and I am sure the others will be glad that you will be there. I'm not entirely sure what is unfolding here, but I feel excited, yet peaceful. I think I am experiencing... joy."

"Wow, err, good. So I'll continue to liaise with Frank and Vanessa and I'll let everyone know when the meeting will be. Don't worry about your dog – he will be welcome, as will Sophie's baby – Vanessa doesn't mind working with children and animals!" he laughed. "Now I must get home; my wife and daughter will be wondering what has happened since I made my last phone call to them."

As Colin locked his door he thought how good it was to have heard Malcolm laugh, but he also wondered why the head was going home so late when there had been no evening meeting at school. And why was he so animated, almost bursting with excitement, at his decision to join the meeting with Vanessa?

Chapter 6 Children and Animals

Vanessa was waiting in the annex to greet them, though she was not the first to turn up that morning; Maria had busied herself very early preparing a snack lunch for them all. She was proud to have had the idea and to have taken the initiative, but rather overwhelmed when Colin pressed a large amount of "lunch fund" cash into her hand with no expectation as to how she should account for it. They had agreed to make this arrangement for the initial meeting, though Maria had plans to create a kitchen budget and to make a nominal charge for refreshments should there be future gatherings.

After her preparations she had returned home to collect Stevie; she had few concerns about her youngest, and had no doubt that she would find him absorbed in front of his games screen; he was used to getting himself dressed before gobbling a breakfast which he normally concocted for himself. Maria hoped to avoid another scene with him at the school gate because she dearly wanted to arrive at the meeting unflustered.

"You'll be a good boy today, won't yer, Stevie? If the teacher tells me you've bin good, me and yer Dad will let yer stay up late to watch the football. But if I 'ave to tell yer Dad you've bin bad, yer know what will happen don't yer?"

"Yes Mum," sighed Stevie, distractedly. He had little idea what it meant to be good or bad, but it hardly mattered because he knew he'd be watching the football anyway; his Dad was bound to let him, and if he was quiet, neither of his parents would notice nor remember what threats or promises they had made. However, Maria need not have worried; Stevie marched into school like a well-trained soldier. She was amazed.

As the group gathered they greeted each other with hugs and brief kisses as though they already enjoyed a close friendship; the relaxed atmosphere and quiet hum of conversation concealed their eager anticipation. Sophie's baby was comfortably surrounded with toys in a play pen which Gabby had rediscovered and brought from home.

"It's a bit old fashioned," she smiled, "but I thought it would be really useful for your little girl to play freely rather than be confined in her buggy."

"I'm so glad you thought of it, thank you. She does look content doesn't she?"

"More so than my daughter who used it thirty years ago," Gabby remarked, sadly. "Sorry, Colin, I don't have anything from my loft store to keep your dog as satisfied as the baby!"

"No worries, Gabby. He'll settle himself down in a corner when he's realised we are staying a while. He doesn't create much fuss these days."

"He looks rather sad," she commented, "is he all right do you think?"

"Perhaps we can help him feel better," interrupted Vanessa. "Colin, will you allow us to heal your dog this morning?"

"Why, yes, thank you. If he receives just a small dose of whatever you gave me, he'll be like a puppy again!"

They chuckled as they moved chairs of all shapes and sizes into a circle.

"Sorry the chairs don't match," said Frank, "me and the kids have been gathering them from all sorts of places. We've cleaned them and they're comfortable, but not terribly elegant. Anyway, there's more than enough. Let's leave space for Malcolm; he'll join us when he's sure the classes are settled."

"They're settled," said Maria, "can't believe how nicely Stevie went in this morning."

"Neither can we!" Frank laughed, "Must have been something to do with Vanessa."

"No it can't be. He hasn't seen her this morning - though he does like you," Maria smiled coyly at Vanessa.

"She doesn't have to be seen to make a difference, do you Vanessa?"

"Now Frank, we're getting a little ahead of ourselves, don't you think? Colin, will you bring your dog to sit close to you within the circle... and we'll start without waiting for Malcolm." Vanessa sounded like a strict school teacher about to begin an important lesson.

She continued, "Thank you all for coming, and many thanks to those of you who have made this room so comfortable for us all. Let me begin by emphasising that we have come together as trustworthy friends, and though our meetings will not contain anything secretive – there'll be no hocus pocus, as some might say - there will be times when we share personal things, safe in the original trust which brought us together.

During our meetings we will discover the underlying cause for our particular way of behaving, and experience how meditation improves our outlook; we will find ways of exploring energies which permeate the universe, though we will not be discovering anything new; in fact, I think you will eventually come to the conclusion that the metaphysical topics we encounter are actually quite natural to you.

You'll understand more when we begin to actively help Colin's dog, but if you already feel uncomfortable with this plan, please feel free to leave and enjoy this beautiful morning, with my love."

The group remained firm, some leaned forward in eager anticipation; there was an air of comfortable confidence in Vanessa's warm compassionate tone.

"Now, let's focus our thoughts upon the dog. Allow your mind to wander freely as you look at him and think about him. Gradually try to filter your thoughts and encourage your mind to choose one word which may describe how the animal feels."

"Sad" said Sophie, immediately.

"Unhappy."

"Tired."

"Lonely."

"Anxious."

They each had a word to contribute. Colin scratched his dog's neck; the animal looked at their faces, aware that the human circle was focussed upon him; and as Malcolm joined the group, he commented, "My God, the dog is feeling his master's emotion."

"How his master *used* to feel," added Colin, firmly.

"Oh, you poor pet," crooned Maria. She fell to her knees, buried her face into the animal's fur and began to cry.

Vanessa reached forward and placed her hand on Maria's shoulder; with gentle firmness she said, "Now Maria, you do not need to share this sadness; let's be free of it shall we?"

"Ok," she sniffed. She stood back to watch as Vanessa moved her hands across the dog's forehead as though smoothing something from his fur. Maria joined in with similar motions, her hands seemingly clearing unwanted stuff from the animal's coat. Slowly the dog moved closer to Vanessa; he rolled over to reveal his belly and she continued a sweeping movement of her hand from the dog's throat to his tail, her palm hovered over the fur without touching his body. Eventually, Maria put her hand near the animal's heart.

"He's feelin' better now ain't he?" she whispered.

"He is. You can feel it through your own heart can't you?" Vanessa murmured.

"It just feels a bit tight, and I want to cry."

"That's because you have taken some of his pain into yourself. Now, just as you did with the dog, move your hand from your heart and sweep it up over your head, like this." She demonstrated as if she was smoothing something away from her face. Maria copied the action, and smiled.

"I'm feelin' all right now."

After a stunned silence the group broke into spontaneous applause. Colin grabbed Maria and hugged her. "Thank you, thank you my dear. I believe you've healed my dog!"

The annex door banged slightly as Malcolm left the room.

Gabby queried, "Vanessa, please explain why Maria did that; why did she apparently know something which the rest of us have no clue about? Because, to be honest, I feel as though I am part of the proverbial 'Emperor's New Clothes' scenario."

"It's difficult to comprehend, I know," replied Vanessa. "What you have seen is a most natural and spontaneous act, where healing hands work upon the body of a creature in need. Maria responded to the situation in a manner which has been practiced throughout history, even though in our evolving world, most have forgotten the skill. Remember how we experience Maria at the school gate? She is used to being her natural self, she doesn't hide behind any adopted personality traits; in fact she's quite authentic."

They smiled.

"So," she continued, "as we began to connect in thought to the dog, Maria's mind was easily able to step aside and allow her true self to do what comes naturally."

"And what is that?" asked Sophie.

"To react spontaneously and compassionately for the ultimate well-being of others," Vanessa replied. "Colin's dog needed help to release the emotional burden he was carrying, and Maria followed her natural instincts to help him to let go of it."

"What exactly was the dog's pain?" queried Gabby.

"I can answer that," Colin blurted. "He and I are so close. When my wife was ill he used to sit by her side and sort of nuzzle against her. She had dementia, you know. When she seemed to be struggling more than usual, he would move closer, and when her hand rested on his fur she seemed to relax and stop...um... struggling..." his voice cracked with emotion. "It seems to me that he sort of took our pain upon himself. I believe you experience something similar, don't you Vanessa? At the school gate you told me that you feel other people's pain. Why is that?"

"It is a consequence of an unusual life encounter which thereafter awakens an insightful connection with the world; for me, there's a deep sensitivity to the emotions, hopes, and sometimes the thoughts of others, which is accompanied by an inner desire to relieve people of their unnecessary suffering, and it becomes natural to desire the well-being of everyone because each individual's state of health affects the welfare of all." Vanessa murmured thoughtfully.

She continued, "Most people relate to a material world where individuals are considered to be separate from each other. However, when we finally discover that we are spiritual beings, we become aware that we are not isolated or detached and we realise that we are part of a greater whole, and so a bond between us is inevitable. It is the spirit at our core which makes it possible to experience the connection with others."

"Ah!" Frank mused. "So it was Maria's naturalness – the way we see her at the gate – which made it easy for her to feel the emotion because she doesn't pretend to be different, special or superior; and, you know, I've heard it suggested that humans have grown farther apart, or forgotten their original connectedness, because our race has evolved with the mistaken idea that we'll ultimately gain by striving to be superior or different, and we have used competition to rise above each other rather than work as one."

For a while the group remained silent as they reflected upon what they had heard.

"Do you have to feel the pain to do this kind of goodness?" Gabby asked. "I would like to be able to help others, but honestly, I've got enough pain of my own without feeling everybody else's."

There was nervous laughter around the group as they empathised with Gabby's vulnerability.

"It's definitely not necessary to feel the pain," Vanessa assured them, "I wouldn't wish that on anybody. Remember how we worked with Colin's dog? When we began to consider the animal's needs, we simply thought about him and found words to help our heart find focus. If your desire is to help, as Gabby said, then your positive loving thought is all that is needed. When you practice such thought you will be amazed at its power."

"Was it your power of thought that had such an unusual effect upon me?" asked Colin.

"And me," added Frank, "I had a similar experience with Vanessa when we left here that day." He glanced around as Malcolm slipped back into his seat while Vanessa leaned back in her chair; she closed her eyes, paused, and then seemed to address the air around her.

"When the spirit within is yearning to be free and ready to be expressed, it leaps with joy when it is openly greeted by another spirit which has already achieved its freedom. It is a meeting of kindred spirits, you might say, though of course we are already closely connected even though we live without awareness of our unity; as Frank commented, throughout our evolution we have forgotten that we are united."

She leaned forward in her seat and looked intently around the group, "We are all One. At the beginning of time we emerged from one great - though small – spirit; it is great in power, though wondrously imperceptible.

Think of it like this: we are like an enormous array of satellite dishes, billions of intricate communicators, situated in a vast desert, constantly sending out inaudible signals into a boundless 'beyond' in search of the infinite; we continually make our connection with 'home' and we're powerfully equipped to receive because our processing mechanics and our communication skills are identical to our source.

Our 'oneness' is magnificent and inexplicable, and so, Colin and Frank, when your spirit found mine, you both experienced a special interaction because of your peak of spiritual readiness; it is an unassailable desire to uncover your connection with the ultimate source of our existence; your beautiful moment of soul engagement caused your mind, emotions, thought and body to become almost completely stilled to allow spirit to come forth."

"Ah," Colin breathed, responding in almost the same trans-like state, "that's why I couldn't move, could hardly breathe and might have fainted. Why did it feel so blissful?"

"Bliss is the continuous state of your spirit," Vanessa explained. "If, for instance, you could move around solely as spirit – without your body, without thinking or feeling – you would feel infinite bliss, for eternity. But that would be rather pointless, wouldn't it?"

"Why pointless? It sounds ideal to me," said Gabby.

"Well, if you continually wandered in a state of bliss, you would never know yourself and you would never experience the journey of life. That's the point of having a body accompanied by thoughts and feelings."

"You mean I am not my body?" asked Malcolm. "Then who or what am I?"

"Such beautiful questions," Vanessa murmured, "you, we, are pure spirit, some would say a soul, choosing a life with a particular body in order to experience something other than bliss."

"But why did Colin and I have this discomforting experience at this particular time?" Frank queried.

"Because, although you did not know it, you were each coming to a state of readiness where your life experiences were approaching breaking point, rather like the bursting of a boil, and your spirit self was ripe to emerge and take control over your mind and emotions. Actually, you both know why this is so, you are aware of the life challenges you have been facing recently, and happily you both attracted me to help burst that proverbial boil."

"So you *do* have an effect on people around you," exclaimed Malcolm, "which explains why the school runs so smoothly when you are around."

"And why Stevie was such a good boy this mornin'," beamed Maria.

"Back to my original thought," mused Gabby, "why can't we all have this effect on others? What is so special about you, Vanessa, and presumably Maria?"

"We are not special," said Vanessa, firmly. "That is, not special in the sense of being important or having unique powers - though we are special in our own ways," she smiled at Maria, "particularly when we accept our relationship with the great power that surrounds us.

Let me use a metaphor about electricity to explain: a light bulb shines within a circuit of electrical energy, and where there is a strong connection to the source of power the bulb shines brightly and consistently; but where there is a frayed wire or loose connection - when the connection to the ultimate power is weak - the bulb flickers and fades."

"And sometimes it's just turned off altogether," sighed Malcolm.

"Though there is always a switch, with someone waiting to help flick it back on," Vanessa raised her eyebrows meaningfully.

Malcolm was swift to change the subject, "Yes, well, um, Vanessa, when Colin and I talked about this meeting, I told him his dog was welcome because you had no fears about working with animals and children. You've attended to the pet, now would you turn your attention to the child? Sophie's baby sounds as though she needs our attention."

Sophie eagerly agreed, "Yes, please, she and I need your loving thought. We have both been miserable recently. My baby always gets upset when I am not at my best; it's a case of like mother, like daughter, I think."

"Wow, don't I know that feeling," muttered Gabby.

"All right then," Vanessa cleared her throat, "first we should make a break between what we have just been discussing and whatever we need to do for Sophie and her baby."

"A comfort break, then," said Frank, "and I could use some water."

"Absolutely. Both are necessary when we are doing spiritual work; our body cleanses out, and then needs replenishing. Take a walk around the room, stretch your body and imagine you are cleaning this space as you swing your arms about, and then take some deep breaths," instructed Vanessa.

"Spring cleanin' the room already?" grinned Maria.

"Something like that, yes. Just like washing hands before eating, we should energetically cleanse before moving on," Vanessa replied.

"It's strange; somehow I understand what she is talking about, yet really I don't have a clue!" exclaimed Gabby.

"Yes, this is all very strange indeed," Colin agreed. "I'm not sure how moving our arms about can make this room 'clean' - not that it was dirty anyway after you ladies gave it your particular attention; and I don't understand how moving hands over my dog can possibly make him feel better, it's not as if they even touched him to give him comfort – although I do sense something remarkably different about him."

"But you just thanked me for healin' your dog!" said Maria indignantly.

"I know I did, my dear; the words just came out of my mouth without thinking."

"Well then, perhaps you should accept what has happened without thinking," said Frank, sternly. "Like you, I can't fathom what it's all about, but I have to believe my own eyes when I see the difference in my wife when she returns from a session with Vanessa. Laura is beginning to understand much more about the process; she talks about how her emotions are a form of 'energy' which affects her body, and she has tried to explain to me how Vanessa somehow has the ability to remove the 'unhealthy' energy so that her body may recover."

"I'm really not sure about all this," said Gabby slowly; she screwed up her eyes and took some deep breaths in an effort to dispel her anxious tears.

Vanessa approached the detached foursome, "Your doubts and concerns do you credit," she said. "I have deep respect for anyone who questions the healing process, and sceptics are always welcome wherever I work. Truth is, it is so very difficult for anyone to explain when words are simply inadequate; nevertheless, given time and opportunity I will do my best to help you to understand as much as possible and to be at peace with that which is unfathomable."

"Thank you," Gabby murmured. "Actually, I sense your sincerity and feel comfortable when you are close to me; perhaps I'm just too used to doubting myself…and look, I'm sorry, I've made everyone wait; please, don't concern yourself with me; let's continue."

Sophie held her baby on her knee as they resumed their seats. The little girl beamed around the circle, she knew that she was the centre of attention.

"Sophie, let her lay on your lap with her head at your knees so that you can hold her feet in your hands," Vanessa instructed. "Now gently begin to massage her toes with your thumbs…then the sides of her feet, down to her heels."

As the instruction continued, Maria suddenly bent down to remove her own socks; lifting one foot onto the opposite knee she began to perform a foot massage upon herself!

Vanessa smiled. "If any of you want to join in, but can't reach your feet," she glanced toward Colin, "you may use one hand to massage the fingers and palm of the other."

"What are we doing?" asked Gabby.

"You may have heard of reflexology?" Frank's wife interrupted. "It's where we connect with the whole of our body. Our feet and our hands are a map of the rest of our body. If we massage parts of our hands or feet, it is as if we are giving ourselves a body massage. You should pay attention to hard places on your sole, or places where the skin is rough; gently give extra attention to these places, and as you massage them, allow your mind its freedom to suggest what part of your body you are tending. For example, at the moment I am kneading the centre pad below my middle toes where it feels as though I am giving my heart some loving attention. And I can find the place which is associated with my breasts; I've been using this method to good effect for my healing needs."

Frank gave Laura's hand a squeeze as his eyes filled with tears.

"But this feels like a personal connection between me and my daughter, not her body," mused Sophie.

"That may also be the case," added Vanessa, "have you noticed how calm you feel."

"Why yes, my heart feels less frantic. Look, this is really nice especially as she is just the right size on my knee, but is it possible to make a similar connection with my son?"

"You may make the same heart communication with *all* your children," replied Vanessa.

57

Sophie gasped in sudden panic; a lump came into her throat as she wondered whether Vanessa was referring to her still-born babies.

"What I mean to say is that it is possible for you all to have powerful heartfelt thought communication with your children and grandchildren. Whatever wisdom you integrate into your own life, you will be able to communicate to the children through your thought connection; indeed, the power of your thought will be effective in shaping their lives for 'highest good' as I like to say," continued Vanessa.

"So you *did* make sure Stevie came to school nicely this morning," exclaimed Maria, in continuing awe of her son's earlier obedience.

"And perhaps you can teach me how I may communicate with my adolescent daughter," added Malcolm making for the door again, "she's sixteen, going on twenty two in her mind, and I fear I'm losing her; she won't even accept a fatherly hug now."

Colin raised his eyebrows; he wondered whether this was the reason for Malcolm's recent stressful outbursts. The canny old man had noted the head's frequent withdrawals from the group; undoubtedly there were occasional needs for him to periodically return to his office, but the manner of his exits appeared to suggest avoidance rather than professional choice. However, Colin found it difficult to associate Malcolm's distracted state with a father's challenges around his adolescent daughter.

"Well," sighed Sophie, "this exercise has made me feel amazingly calm, and see, she is so contented, even though it must be time for her feed."

"You have a beautiful, sensitive daughter," murmured Vanessa, "you and your husband have done well to produce two healthy children, and yes, I'm sure it's time for us all to enjoy the food Maria has prepared."

Their lunch was shared in a relaxed atmosphere where they chatted as if they had been together for a long time.

"You know, we really must do this again; surely we can come together on a regular basis?" Gabby suggested. "I have so many questions, there is so much more I want to know and learn, and I think that if I get a grip on what Vanessa has to teach I can be a better, even happier person."

"I feel the same," said Frank, "and I gather the way is clear for us to use this annex room whenever we like."

"That's great, we are lucky to have such a comfortable place to meet, but we ought to have a meaningful name rather than 'the annex'. I was thinking about using the first letters of Spiritual Healing Energy Domain and calling it our SHED," she replied.

"Very clever," Colin responded, "though our room is not very shed-like; don't we need something spectacular or adventurous like Enterprise or Endeavour?"

"Um, those sound like names people would choose for a business centre, and that's not what we want, though since our explorations are beyond the earth, I was wondering about other space objects, for example, 'Sputnik'; does anyone know what it means?" asked Frank.

"You mean the first satellite into space, launched by Russia in 1957?"

"Well remembered, Colin, yes."

"Well, our room is a kind of satellite, set apart from the school and village," mused Gabby.

"I was thinking about the literal translation of Sputnik; it means 'fellow traveller.' We are fellow travellers of earth trying to make sense of our journey and discovering wisdom of the ages through Vanessa. No doubt we'll want our children to know about all this, and their children too. It will be our tradition, our lore - Sputnik's Lore!" Frank declared dramatically.

"That has an unusual and amazing ring to it," Colin commented, "it's just right! Sputnik's Lore: Spiritual Lessons for a school gate committee."

"School gate committee? What's that? I don't want to be on no committee," muttered Maria.

Malcolm called from the doorway where he had been standing unnoticed for some time: "It's like this, Maria; parents who linger after school are sometimes referred to as the school gate committee. They can be a teacher's dilemma, or a head-teacher's nightmare."

"I don't know about the first, but I'm definitely the head-teacher's nightmare."

They burst into laughter; Maria hadn't yet realised how amusing and clever she could be.

Chapter 7   Father Figure

"I don't know where she can be," Sophie fretted, "she's been really looking forward to this meeting, in fact driving Maria and me to distraction with her eagerness to have answers to her many questions. We left here late yesterday after she was sure everything was prepared. She likes things to be perfect, so she'll be very upset about being late. What can have happened to her?"

The "Sputnik" group had created an agenda for another meeting from "Gabby's list" as they affectionately called it, but their chief enquirer was missing.

"Perhaps she's decided not to join us after all," said Colin. "She and I were talking in the village the other day; we shared thoughts about the meetings and came to the conclusion that we both have doubts and feel bemused. She told me she'd lain awake thinking about Maria's actions with my dog and the subsequent discussion about what it meant; she said she'd become convinced that it was all nonsense and decided that she'd stay away, but having made that decision she recalled how peaceful she felt and how she really wanted to be here to know more; we agreed that we both have feelings which fluctuate between keen interest and total incredulity."

"Well, that's true," said Sophie slowly, "Gabby and I have had lots of discussions with Maria trying to make sense of what she did, and the three of us came to the conclusion that it is impossible to understand what occurred. We have come to know Maria really well, we trust her, and we believe that what happened came spontaneously from her heart; anyway Colin, whatever she did appeared to make things better for you and your dog."

"Indeed it did," replied Colin pensively, "which is why I'm here once more; but where is Gabby, and why is she not here with us?"

Vanessa joined in their discussion, "I totally understand your doubts and really appreciate your willingness to share how you feel," she said with a warm smile. "Perhaps you'll allow me to show you all how to handle this uncertainty?

Please settle yourself into your chair, sit quietly and begin to concentrate on breathing; listen to each breath as it moves through your body – in, and out; pay attention to every breath; focus upon the rise and fall of your abdomen as you breathe in and out…

Initially, this sustained concentration is quite challenging, but be patient and keep your attention upon the rise and fall of your stomach; try not to change the way you breathe, simply watch and notice how your body takes care of it for you…

Now centre your thought upon Gabby; repeat her name a few times in your mind. Try not to imagine where she is, or wonder what may have happened, just think of her.

Now turn your attention to your chest, the place where your heart is located, but rather than thinking about your beating heart, imagine this space is filled with billowing pink cloud."

"Like candy floss," murmured Maria.

"Just like candy floss; imagine it expanding from your chest, and as you focus upon the image, notice how the pink continues to grow out from your heart; imagine scooping out a portion from the fluffy mass, and as you hold the piece in the palm of your hand, visualise sending it to Gabby."

"I'm blowing mine into the wind, straight from my heart to hers," said Laura. "It's coming from what's called our heart chakra isn't it?"

"It is," affirmed Vanessa. "The energy centres associated with our body are called chakras; there are many of them throughout the body located strategically along pathways or circuits of vitality; it's not easy to explain their presence because they cannot be seen, which is why the system is called the subtle body. Most texts on 'Eastern Thought' focus upon seven chakras positioned vertically through the body from the base of the spine to the crown; I recommend that you read about them to gain some basic knowledge, but essentially you should explore them for yourself for there is nothing better than learning from inner wisdom."

"Please explain how we do that," said Malcolm.

"Well, we're still awaiting Gabby's arrival, so this is not the right time for us to explore our chakras extensively, but you can discover them for yourself by following these instructions…"

Vanessa paused to adjust herself to a more upright position in her chair; she removed her shoes and placed her feet firmly on the floor.

"Is it important to be seated in such a specific way?" interrupted Colin.

"It makes me feel firmly balanced in my body," she replied patiently, "my feet feel firmly 'planted' on the ground; my spine is straight, though relaxed, and I'm in a position to easily access the features I want to talk to you about..."

"All right; I understand, yes, please continue."

She smiled at his efforts to precisely follow her guidance and at his long-term habit of needing to control important meetings, both idiosyncrasies resulting from a lifetime of perfectionist leadership; and she compassionately understood that another's direct and overbearing manner often concealed their immense fear.

She cleared her throat and began her instruction, "Choose a time when you feel contentedly relaxed and when you are sure you will not be disturbed; sit comfortably with your spine as straight as possible and focus upon your breathing, just as we did a few minutes ago when we sent our thought to Gabby.

Close your eyes and place the palm of your hand on your body over the location of each chakra:

First, at the lowest point of your spine where your 'base' chakra is located - it does not matter whether you place your hand on your back or at the front of your body, but keep your hand still while you focus upon your breathing.

Now, move your hand onto your stomach – your second chakra - just below your navel, and rest your palm there for a few moments while you continue to notice each breath.

Next, rest your palm on the space above your navel, this is called your solar plexus; continue to breathe steadily and pause with your hand gently resting there.

Now move on to your heart and allow your hand to rest at the centre of your chest; by now you ought to be quite relaxed by being attentive to your breathing.

After a while place your hand at your throat, which is your fifth chakra, then move your hand to rest at your forehead;

and finally place your palm on your crown chakra which is at the top of your head.

Practice this procedure several times during each seated quiet time; try to be open to allow freedom of thought as your hand rests upon each chakra position so that ideas and images guide your awareness."

"I don't think I'm enough in tune with my thoughts for this," remarked Colin, "could you give us some clues?"

Vanessa smiled, "As I explained, the chakras are aspects of your subtle body, so it is not easy to uncover them, and it takes time and practice to develop focussed attention to all parts of your body and mind. However, while we wait for Gabby I'll offer some 'clues' as you say.

When we were thinking about Gabby a few moments ago, we briefly explored the heart chakra, so let's continue to investigate it. Most people are happy to differentiate between their beating heart and a functional emission of love and compassion which they believe comes from the similar space; the former is our physical organ, and the emotional energy comes from the latter, the heart chakra. You may like to try a simple exercise based upon this chakra:

As we practiced earlier: close your eyes, place the palm of your right hand on your chest and be attentive to your breathing. Now imagine that your heart is like a beautiful flower ready to open its petals."

"Mine's a lily," said Laura softly, her expression serene.

"And I think mine could be a rose," added Frank, "I mean a winter rose just peeking through the snow."

"Whatever you see, or whatever you choose, focus your thought upon your flower's centre as it opens to reveal an avenue leading within."

"Like bees going into a snapdragon," suggested Sophie.

"Exactly. And now as you continue your breath-work, your flower bursts open, petals fall and your beautiful inner light shines out to the world. Imagine that each time you breathe out you shower those around you with love, and with each inward breath, love is drawn into your heart."

"That's lovely," whispered Maria. "I'll remember this and explain it to Gabby the next time she comes to my house."

"I'm sure you'll discover lots of images to explain to Gabby and many more people in the future," smiled Vanessa. "But for now, let's briefly reconsider another of these energy centres:

Once again, place your hand back on your tummy, the space below your navel,"

"My second chakra," said Sophie.

"Yes, and it is also called the energy centre of your emotions; undoubtedly, you will have experienced emotional turmoil in your stomach, for example when you've been anxious, frightened or angry; this is because the chakra which enables us to control our emotions is in the same location as your stomach."

"And can we actually *control* our emotions?" asked Malcolm intently.

"We can. If, for example, you are disposed to bouts of anger, and are determined to control its outward explosive effect, you should focus upon this space below your navel; when you feel the onset of anger, breathe with a slow and steady rhythm as if each deep breath comes from your stomach," she smiled encouragingly.

"And will that really work?" asked Colin, archly.

"If it doesn't, I'll have you beside me to remind me to be calm!" retorted Malcolm with a grin.

Ignoring their playful interruption, Laura continued with her serious enquiry, "Is there a chakra corresponding to the place where the body's 'T' cells are created? I need to focus on these to help my body during some treatment which I must have."

"Yes, this is the base chakra, located, as I said earlier, at the bottom of your spine; it is the energy centre tuned to the physical body. Use the palm of your hand as we have already practiced to focus your attention at this lowest point of your body; take some steady deep breaths as if you are breathing in and out of the chakra; when your eyes are closed you may see a hint of red in your mind's eye because this is the colour associated with the base chakra, and indeed, a focus upon the energy of red would be good for you, Laura."

"What about the forehead, a place which seems to fascinate people who are used to the idea of chakras?" Laura persisted.

"The centre of the forehead is known as the 'third eye'; this space is often explored with the mistaken belief that psychic perception can be activated by persistent contemplation upon this point. For me, meditating with focus upon this chakra leads to deep introspection rather than attempted precognition," Vanessa responded, dryly.

"You're not interested in psychic phenomena such as predicting someone's future, then?" Colin's tone hinted at disapproval.

"I prefer to use spiritual wisdom to learn more about myself and my place in the world, and my desire is to help others do the same;" she replied, "and wherever extra-sensory ability helps this goal I am happy to use it, but I choose not to seek it simply as a curiosity."

"But you do have a sense of someone's past...or future?" he persisted.

"Each person must come to terms with issues from their past, and my work usually helps the important process of forgiveness; and of course, each of us has complete freedom of choice about our future," she responded, firmly.

"May we get back to learning about chakras?" interrupted Malcolm, irritably.

"Of course," Vanessa replied. "I realise we've moved right away from our original agenda, although by returning to the topic of chakras it is possible to keep to the subject of today's meeting by giving further brief attention to the space I described earlier as the solar plexus, located in your middle, below your chest.

This subtle body connection is our centre of self-esteem; it is here that people who are challenged by their lack of self-worth feel defeated and many experience symptoms such as indigestion. When the breathing techniques I have mentioned are used to focus upon this space, it is possible to enhance self-belief and powerfully shine from one's centre just as the solar title suggests."

She added, "Please be aware that our spontaneous discussion has overlooked some chakras, and those we have mentioned contain much more detail, but this brief encounter will help you to discover centres upon which to focus as you grow in self-understanding.

For now, let's return our focus upon our heart. Once again, imagine your breath enters and then emerges from your heart...in and out of your heart...and by this action we send the power of loving thought from our heart chakra to Gabby. There. She will know our particular thought is with her – sent and received at the speed of thought!

And finally we allow the resolution of her problem to unfold while we focus once more upon our breathing."

"Well, I don't know what's happened to Gabby, but the breathing exercise has really made me feel peaceful, surprisingly peaceful," sighed Colin. "Thank you, Gabby wherever you are."

"I'm here," came an anxious voice from the door, "just arrived... didn't know whether to come in because you were so quiet... been an awful morning... argument with my daughter because she was supposed to do the school run today and she forgot... unpleasant text from hubby... car wouldn't start... lost my house keys... fell over the doorstep and grazed my knee... look I've torn my tights and bruised my wrist... broke my phone so I couldn't call you Sophie; and I so wanted to be here..."

"And now you are!" Sophie murmured.

"I'll get some first aid stuff," busied Maria.

Gabby had been capable and strong during her unfolding difficulties, but having finally arrived at the meeting she became overwhelmed by the group's care and compassion. In tears she sounded like a little girl, "I so wanted to be here, there was lots I wanted to know, I want to be a better person, I should be the one to be caring, no-one ever cares for me, I want to be happy, I do so want to be happy," she wailed.

"Look, how about the rest of us disappear for a while so that Gabby can have some private time with Vanessa? Laura and I would be glad to have you in our home. How does that sound?" suggested Frank.

"It sounds awful," Gabby's childlike wail continued. "I know sometimes I've been undecided about our meetings, but actually I learned a lot when Colin shared with us, and when we thought about his dog, and the baby, and anyway we discuss things together in here, don't we? I don't want you all to go, I want me and Vanessa to work together and have everyone learn together, including you, Malcolm. I don't want you to run away just at the moment when we are doing something good. Oh! I wish I could do something good."

"You want a lot of things," grinned Frank.

"And a few home truths are escaping through your tears too," added Colin. "Are you all right, Malcolm?"

"I am. And she's right. Sometimes this stuff becomes overwhelming for me, and I want to run; but you must have noticed I do return. The magnet of love pulls me back."

"What a lovely thing to say," smiled Gabby, gradually breathing her distress away. "May we begin, Vanessa?"

"I think we already have! Let's have an early refreshment break and return to our circle in a while."

71

Eager to hear Vanessa's thoughts on the reasons for Gabby's tormented morning, they settled back into their chairs. Vanessa closed her eyes, and with deep, measured breaths she began: "You will be familiar with the phrase: 'spirit is willing, though the flesh is weak.' It is an expression which Gabby may have used for herself this morning: her spirit was thrilled at the prospect of our meeting while her physical self apparently experienced many struggles on the way here.

However, as we learn about Gabby's everyday difficulties, it will become clear that this expression does not apply to her; in fact, like most of us, Gabby has internal struggles which occur because the body is strong and determined, and the mind and emotions have an even stronger power of control, especially when they are resolute; so, in actual fact, it is clear that the spirit may be overcome. This morning's incidents were caused by a conflict between Gabby's strong emotions and her expectant spirit, and the battle played out through her material world."

"Wasn't it just one of those bad days when it would have been better to have stayed in bed because nothing was going right, and in such situations you know that the harder you try, the worse the day tends to become," suggested Malcolm.

"That's how it appears," agreed Vanessa, "though when you understand the cause of such events you will in future be able to stop any potential downward spiral and improve your day. You see, these situations occur when your earthly self is not in agreement with your spirit, and then it can seem as if the whole universe has conspired against you."

"But I really did want to be here today," interrupted Gabby, "and as you said, my spirit wanted me to be here too, because we are learning spiritual things aren't we?" Her pleas continued to sound like those of a small child.

"Everyone knows how much you want to learn," soothed Vanessa, "you are a shining light amongst us."

Satisfied, Gabby settled to listen as Vanessa continued. "Consciously Gabby made her decision and desperately wanted to be at this meeting, and her spirit had the same desire because its ultimate aim is for Gabby to live according to spiritual direction - doing good, as she would say. However, another aspect of Gabby – her worldly self – had fearful concerns about a potential major life change, and may well have thought: 'We're all right as we are, something new might be threatening, and we want to feel safe; life is not very happy, but at least it's what we know.' This worldly self in all of us, sometimes called the ego, acts according to our personal desires, thoughts and emotions, and when faced with novel situations it sometimes reacts like a frightened child, and that's why we heard Gabby's frightened childlike voice.

We have all experienced these problematic days when, as Malcolm suggests, it would be easier to give up, but we stumble on with increased fear and trepidation; our already fragile connection with spirit is lost and we become disorientated because we no longer have any centre of calm;

consequently we attract more problems which seem to suggest we are careless and accident prone, and subsequently, as our disasters continue, we convince ourselves that we are on the wrong path."

"Like one of those Friday the thirteenth days?" suggested Maria.

"Only if you're superstitious!" Frank grinned.

Vanessa ignored their comments and continued, "As I've suggested, Gabby's earthly self – her ego - would have been pleased if she had not made it to our meeting; her absence from such a spiritual gathering would have ensured that spirit remained undiscovered and therefore a subsequent change in her personal life would have been unlikely; ego's plan may have ensured that her unhappy state continued, and after all, Gabby's earthly self probably thinks an unhappy life is what she deserves because that is how it has always been, and because of low self-esteem she believes that this is what she should expect for her future. My explanation suggests that this morning's outer world experiences reveal Gabby's ongoing inner turmoil."

"I find this preposterous," said Colin, irritably. "You're suggesting that we consist of separate aspects which behave independently? Surely it is our intellect which controls what we do and how we think; we know our own mind don't we? What do you mean when you say there needs to be an inner agreement, and how can this be achieved?"

"We are very complex beings," said Vanessa gently. "Our spirit is what I call our natural self, the part that carries on from one lifetime to another; it is the part that Gabby wants to be in touch with most – she wants to learn about spirituality. However, we also have other aspects of our self, each having an agenda of what might be possible to achieve through life: our desiring self - our will - wants certain successes, our emotional self wants to experience a plethora of feelings, and these are clustered around a body which becomes a stage on which to play our life's agenda.

The most important thing for us to learn from Gabby's eventful morning is that we can alter the course of such a day, or better still, prevent a catalogue of disasters from happening in the first place by ensuring that our earthly self is in communion with our soul's agenda; with soul and body in harmony our life progresses more smoothly, despite the inevitable ups and downs."

"If that is so, how can we be so distrusting or dismissive of our spirit or soul?" Colin persisted.

"How indeed! It happens because we have forgotten who we are. We've lost touch with our true self because we have forgotten the art of setting aside time to be still in order to listen to our soul. Frequently we've been told that we are worthless individuals undeserving of success, our self-esteem is crushed, and we accept criticism rather than taking control of our lives as powerful, spirit beings."

"That's exactly how my life has been. May I tell you some things about me?" asked Gabby.

Vanessa smiled her encouragement. She understood the diversity of need within the group: some were able to receive her love with just an awed gaze, while others had to explain the minutiae of their lives before they could accept her healing. "I expect you have things to share about your relationship with your father."

"Yes. How did you know? Ever since I can remember my father has criticised me; in fact, till the day he died I struggled to achieve anything that would please him. He commented on my hair, my figure, my clothes; he found fault with my school work even when teachers said it was fine; he disliked my boyfriends and regularly told me I was no good. I don't know what I did wrong to cause him to dislike me so much. And now I don't know why I am telling you all," she finished wearily.

"You're giving yourself an explanation for the meticulous way you have to keep your home; you're explaining why you need your family to do the right thing in your eyes, and you are helping yourself to understand why you and your husband have separated," Vanessa explained gently. "My dear Gabby, throughout your life you have been striving for what seemed unattainable – to receive praise and unconditional love; you never received this from your father, and so your mind decided that the way to gain acknowledgement was through keeping an orderly home, whilst your emotional self attempted to grasp loving respect by trying to make a 'good' family. Sadly, even though aspects of yourself have been doing all they can to make things better for you, their plan is hopeless."

"Ah," breathed Colin, "her independent parts want the best for her, but have not asked her soul for its wisdom."

"Exactly"

"Thank you for your account, Gabby; your struggles confirm for me how we all waver," he murmured; and with hesitation he pondered, "So, Vanessa, this is what we can expect when our mind and emotions are strong and our spirit remains hidden and ignored?"

"It is. Every day most of us are used to paying attention to our thoughts and opinions, and many – especially women, I might add – are familiar with responding to emotion; usually if your gut feeling tells you 'no', you will not venture into something new."

"That's it!" exploded Gabby, "I felt an inner conflict between my mind which wanted to avoid today's meeting and my emotions which were excited at the prospect of attending."

"And your excitement was so huge your mind became even more reticent," added Sophie.

"And both parts didn't take notice of your spirit which definitely wanted you to be 'ere!" squealed Maria.

"So you nearly didn't arrive, and almost sabotaged your greatest need – to do the perfect, good thing." Vanessa concluded.

And for once Gabby did not mind being the subject of laughter.

Maria suddenly pushed her chair away from the circle and hurried to the kitchen. Her sensitivity to the needs of her friends was rapidly unfolding and she became confident of her role in providing the most appropriate meals and snacks at the most suitable time. The group quickly learned to trust her wisdom and followed her lead when she indicated a break was necessary. Her healthy food choices were appreciated though she often chose unusual combinations and insisted that they ate dishes in a particular order. Her decisions were a mystery to the group and to herself, though the conversations about her menus gave light relief to the otherwise heavy topics of the day:

"Why must I eat fruit first?" moaned Colin, "I prefer it as my dessert."

"Because I said so," muttered Maria.

"And why must I have banana, and Frank has to have pineapple?"

"Because I said so."

"And why does Laura have to eat so many sweet red peppers with her salad? Because you said so?"

"I don't know why, all right?" she shouted.

"Colin, she knows because she knows, all right?" interrupted Vanessa with a doting smile on them all.

Gabby's challenges earlier in the day made her forget many of her questions, though after their meal Vanessa focussed their thought once more:

"I'd like you all to really take to heart what Gabby's experience has illustrated for us today. Firstly, you should understand the significance of the connection between the emotions you express or repress and the corresponding reactions of your body. For example, I am sure you know how your body reacts when you face something important like a test, an exam or an interview?"

"The anxiety and fear makes your heart race, your body sweat and your hands shake," said Malcolm.

"You've neatly described the connection. When you feel something intensely, the emotion becomes apparent through your body. There is a constant connection between your emotions and your body, and this is the cause of illness: sweaty palms and shaking hands can also become heart disease, skin irritation, or any other disease whenever uncontrolled and aggravating emotions are allowed to persist."

"You mean, my feelings make me ill?" murmured Laura.

"The connection is real, Laura, but not in the judgemental way you fear. You have not 'made' yourself sick." Vanessa said, softly. "But you will appreciate how powerful our mind and emotions are when their effect is so tangible. However, when given its freedom, our spirit actually *is* stronger than our mind and body, and when spirit is allowed to work through the energy of your thought, as I have said, you will be amazed at its power."

"How do we sort ourselves out then?" asked Maria.

"By becoming wise to the mind and body connection – psychoneuroimmunology is its scientific term."

"What do you mean by becoming wise to it?" asked Frank.

"Let me give you an example: Imagine you're happily driving your car when a vehicle from behind overtakes dangerously, then squeezes between you and a car in front so that you have to brake violently. Perhaps the errant driver repeats his performance causing disruption to queues ahead until all vehicles have to stop at traffic lights. How might you feel and how might you behave?"

"Really angry; perhaps swear at him."

"So irritated, I'd hold my hand on the car horn and deliberately try to squeeze him out of the queue."

"I'd be upset and reach to lock my car door in case there was trouble at the traffic lights."

"Yes, most of us would have those kinds of angry or fearful emotions, causing us to behave erratically, and as a result our physical body is damaged."

"From an accident?"

"Perhaps; though I was thinking of the damage of increased heart rate and elevated blood pressure as a result of anger, and nausea and headache due to anxiety."

"But these are natural reactions," said Malcolm, "anger erupts every day of the week."

"Indeed it does," said Vanessa, meaningfully. "So what do you suppose is happening to your body when, as you say, your anger erupts every day of the week?"

"Umm. I guess I'm setting myself up for a heart attack," Malcolm muttered, humbly.

"So what should we angry people do?" asked Maria, expertly saving Malcolm's face.

"In the immediacy of the situation, notice what is happening to you; pause and realise that anger is rising and that you're in danger of behaving 'angrily'; take deep breaths into the seat of your anger - your stomach - and diffuse its energy by slowly breathing out of your mouth; allow others to behave as they choose and avoid becoming embroiled in unnecessary reactions.

After the event, when you have had time to reconsider, ask yourself *why* another person's behaviour brought forth your anger because, in truth, the *actual reason* for your strong emotion is usually unrelated to the incident which caused it," Vanessa explained.

"How interesting," mused Colin, glancing towards Malcolm. "And is it likely that, when faced with similar situations, our angry reaction will be repeated until we, say, have a heart attack?"

"Or until we respond to our wise self, which will inwardly guide us towards the moment when we acknowledge the real reason for our disquiet," said Vanessa, firmly.

"That moment may be quite scary," Malcolm muttered as he dropped his chin on to his chest with a trembling sigh.

"But it's good to have the support of wise friends if you feel you're living with the potential of an emotional outburst," added Colin, thoughtfully.

"Oh dear," sighed Gabby, anxiously, "analysing and understanding myself is very daunting; these ideas are so difficult to grasp."

"Well, step by step, you are all learning," Vanessa continued, "and you will be surprised how different you feel even by being a member of this group; you see, your inner self, your subconscious mind is alert and paying attention to everything here; and that is why it was wonderful that

Gabby so wisely asked everyone to remain while she explained what has been happening in her life."

"You are most welcome; and you know, I want to say this: I love you all very much; you are like a family to me, and our secure relationship has blossomed so incredibly quickly; in future I'll try not to be so doubtful."

"We are glad to have your love, Gabby, though actually I would like to go on to mention a second immensely important piece of wisdom which we can learn as a result of hearing about your difficulties."

"I'm surprised I only have two things to learn," she said ruefully.

Vanessa smiled. "We must cultivate, nurture and value self-esteem. Let me assure you, the burden that we carry, and the root of most of our difficulties, is low self-esteem; when we change this in ourselves and in our children we will have performed a wonderful 'miracle'. In fact, by arranging these meetings you have created a perfect opportunity to bring to life an incredible vision for yourself and for members of our community."

She concluded their gathering by speaking with an intensity they had not previously encountered, "Indeed, you are truly a blessing for mankind."

Chapter 8   Sputnik's Lore

Colin liked to exercise his mind as well as his body, and he spent the next few days writing as much as he could remember of Vanessa's words. He rarely stayed at home, preferring to work, eat and chat in "Sputnik's Hub".

"What yer writing?" Maria called from the kitchen where she had successfully served another soup lunch.

"Well, ever since our last meeting I've been thinking about Vanessa's words. She was so very intense in her desire for us to grasp the importance of self-esteem, it is obviously crucial to our understanding of 'who we are' as she would say; so I thought I'd write down my thoughts in small chunks so that the ideas are easy for me to remember and apply to my life."

"I can't help yer I'm afraid. She loses me when she starts talkin' with her eyes closed; I like to get stuck in and do things without thinkin'.

Look, here's Laura! She's good at art; p'raps she'll copy your words nicely, then you could stick the paper on the wall so that everyone can see it."

"What a marvellous idea, Maria, you really are 'in touch' you know."

"More like 'touched' the way I feel these days. I mean touched in the 'ead like. My hubby don't get what I'm on about, but that's all right, so long as his tea's on the table he's 'appy.

Now then Laura, we're glad you've come; please could you talk to Colin so I can get cleared up?"

Laura and Colin grinned; they were delighted to see how Maria had discovered her niche within the group; it was clear that her attitude to life and her confidence around others had significantly changed; she had become their lively example of the positive effect of self-esteem.

"What are you up to, Colin?" Laura asked as she struggled to reach for her chair; she was clearly in considerable pain.

"Never mind about me, dear Laura, what about you? It grieves me to see you like this. What can you tell me about it?"

"I'm off work now, Colin, taking medication as well as exploring alternative therapies, and of course I'm having healing sessions with Vanessa. It will be all right in the end."

"Of course it will. Rest assured the group will be a continual support for you, Frank and the children until your problem is resolved. We will be so pleased, proud and relieved when you beat this."

Laura's chin dropped, and as she shuffled herself upright in her chair she replied, "I'm not beating this. There is nothing to fight. I am neither at war with my body nor the disease. It will not become the preoccupying topic in my family's life. It is simply a part of my journey which I am learning to embrace, and then move through."

There was applause at the door from Malcolm who had perfected the habit of choosing strategic moments to listen in to the conversation of others; he walked into the room, Colin stood up, and Maria rushed from the kitchen to acknowledge Laura's wisdom and determination. The four united in a long embrace until Malcolm, remembering the actual reason for his arrival, broke away,

"Sorry to change the subject, but I'm here hunting for Stevie; he took off again, Maria. Something got under his skin and he ran; I thought he may have come to find you."

"I'm 'ere," came a small voice from under the table. "I came in when you were all kissin'"

"You are a naughty boy, Stevie. You scare me and the teachers when you run off."

"Didn't run off, I just 'scaped."

"Escaped from where Stevie?" asked his head-teacher.

"From class. It's a cage; I 'ate it in there and I 'ate you."

Malcolm knelt on the floor in front of the little boy. "Tell me what's happened, and together we'll try to work it out so you don't hate so much."

Stevie's morning had been crammed with disasters: he couldn't understand what the teacher expected him to do, children had laughed at him, he couldn't figure out how to hold his pencil, he'd lost his reading book and his lunch had disappeared.

"Let's begin with the last problem, Stevie. I am sure your Mum has got some soup left over from lunch. Sit at the table and eat here."

Malcolm returned to the school building to address the rest of the little boy's problems which seemed to centre upon the ethos of the reception class; Colin and Laura resumed their paperwork while Stevie wriggled in his chair trying to adjust to an adult meal table: "You could make this soup taste better, Mum."

"Well, you little, ungrateful…"

"How could the soup be made better?" interrupted Colin, "What would you do with it?"

"Put some of them clover leaves in it."

"You mean water cress."

"Cress, yes"

"Anything else?"

"Put some cheese on the top."

"And?"

"Some of those bits of bread."

"Croutons, I believe you mean." Laura and Colin suppressed their smiles as Maria plonked herself next to her son with her eyes gaping.

"Where did you get those fancy ideas?"

"Telly. I like watching food programmes when you and Dad are at work."

"That's when you should be asleep; I'll 'ave the plug taken off that TV. I'll 'ave a word with yer Dad…"

"What would you like to be when you grow up, Stevie?" Colin interrupted again.

"A chef."

Malcolm returned to join the end of another conversation, "Well, young man, we will have to give you some practice. I think there will be times when you may come in here and visit your Mum. Perhaps she will give you chef's jobs like arranging the table or carrying out the fruit. But chefs have to read their recipes, so you will need to pay special attention to everything your teacher tells you, and I am sure she will be asking you to write and draw your favourite foods – very soon, in fact this afternoon. So off you go and say sorry to her for escaping from the cage."

The adults' laughter erupted as Stevie left the room.

"Self-esteem," chuckled Colin, "miracles will occur when you receive a boost to your self-esteem! He'll be reading so quickly now you've given him a good reason to tackle the mystery.

Now Malcolm, do you have time to read a paper which Laura and I have been considering? I want to create a type of 'mission statement' to help dispel low self-esteem, and this is it…"

Sputnik's Lore: Accepting Ourselves

We own our idiosyncrasies and personality traits which tend to make us anxious; our acceptance means we avoid saying, 'I wish I was different.'

We recognise that even though we possess these traits, it is possible for us to learn ways of reducing their impact and even be free of them completely.

We understand that the journey of accepting these difficulties and taking steps to be free of them is an opportunity to learn lessons for life.

We will be kind to ourselves especially throughout our difficult experiences.

We have the wisdom not to dwell upon our difficulties, nor speak about them in ways which cause them to be reinforced.

Whether our difficulties continue or whether we become completely
free of them makes no difference to who we are.
We love our self 'just as we are.'

We appreciate others when they love us 'just as we are' because it
helps us all to be free from the additional stress of trying to create a
perfect relationship.
We pay attention to our self before looking for ways to care for
others.
The behaviour of others towards us does not affect who we are.
We recognise that the challenging behaviour of others may be the
result of their difficulties of self-acceptance.
We allow others to behave as they choose without any expectation
of how we think they ought to behave.
We allow others to behave as they choose while maintaining our
own self-acceptance.
We understand that the journey of life is an adventure of the heart
and soul.
We see the light of the inner spirit of everyone; it is Love.

"Uum. I appreciate the work you've put into this, Colin, though your phrases may be a little intense for some people to grasp. However, the work you have done here, together with Stevie's troubles today, have made me think more seriously about how we may construct a curriculum which will bring Vanessa's teaching to the hearts and minds of our children," said Malcolm.

"Sputnik's Lore for life?" suggested Laura, "Though honestly, Malcolm, my children are being perfectly educated through your school and, despite Stevie's misgivings and some little blips in today's reception class, the school really does have a good ethos."

"True," responded Malcolm, "and believe me I am grateful for your confidence in my school. We have a new reception teacher who definitely needs more of my support, but generally we create an ethos where children's gifts are valued, where they are encouraged to strive to achieve their best, where they are praised for their efforts and rewarded for achievement. However, I have a sense that Vanessa's teaching goes far beyond our philosophy, so I would like to hear what she has to say in the weeks ahead, and then maybe together we can offer a workshop for our teachers and parents."

"And what about the kids who have left your school?" Maria interrupted. "My lot at home could do with learnin' about self-esteem."

"Indeed they could, Maria," he replied. "We must look into providing interest here for the teenagers in our community. Lord knows, I have a daughter at home who could do with some advice, and I don't seem to be the one who can give it."

"Fathers are often not the best teachers for adolescents," smiled Laura, "but I know that Frank will be very interested in leading the youngsters in this kind of project; he'd be good at it, and he's going to need something to keep his mind occupied in the weeks ahead," she added distractedly.

"Is this a fringe meeting? May anyone join?" called Sophie as she appeared at the door. "My mother-in-law has my daughter for the afternoon; I ought to be getting housework done, but I couldn't resist coming to see if anything was going on here."

"Your housework can be done anytime," laughed Colin, "you have your priorities right by joining us! Have a look at something I've been working on here; Malcolm thinks my ideas are rather intense, but setting them down on paper has helped me understand Vanessa's teaching a little better."

Sophie joined them at the table. "Your statements are nicely short, and they make a good reminder list, but I'm not sure the thinking has gone far enough to help us through our challenges. What I mean is, I can't believe it's simply self-esteem that Vanessa wants us to grasp; perhaps the concept is just a small step towards something more that she has to teach us?   It's true that good educators like you and Malcolm know the destructive impact of low self-esteem and, to be sure, I've been feeling the damaging power of worthlessness as a result of my ex-friend's behaviour towards me, but I don't think Vanessa's plan is just to remind us to feel good about ourselves in our relationship with our friends... and enemies."

"Well, you may like to ask her yourself," said Colin, who had spotted Vanessa making her way towards the building.

"No, not now," Sophie replied, "such an important discussion can wait until we are all together."

Vanessa greeted them with a hug, "You look as though you are all intent upon something significant," she remarked. "I'm glad because your discussions affect everyone else; in fact, each time an individual makes progress in personal growth, their success becomes part of evolution, and it is felt by all."

"All this talkin' is hard for me," complained Maria, "I think I'm gonna be left out."

"Believe me, Maria," said Malcolm as he put his arm around her, "you, out of all of us, are not the one to be left behind, though I do think it's a shame we have to wait for another gathering when we are making such progress right now."

"Well, we can continue, if you like," suggested Vanessa, "you are all eager, and though we are missing Gabby and Frank, I expect they will be here soon."

Frank and Gabby opened the door and were greeted by squeals and laughter.

"Now what's going on?" grinned Frank.

"I'm constantly surprised at the appropriate timing of people's arrival through that door," spluttered Colin.

"And why should that surprise you?" declared Maria with a knowing glance towards her mentor, "Vanessa told us about the amazin' power of thought; our heart called out to them, and 'ere they are!"

Gabby and Frank perused the written statements as they all settled into their comfortable chairs.

"Honestly Colin, I'm stunned at your work," cried Gabby, "especially after you told me you thought we ought to be cautious about accepting everything we discover here: 'All is not what it seems,' was what you said to me the other day."

"Well, just like you, I have second thoughts," he said smothering his embarrassment with a cough, and with growing concern about Vanessa's opinion of him he asked, "Are *you* pleased with my work, my dear?"

Vanessa, seemingly oblivious to Colin's discomfort, warmly congratulated him on his step-by-step affirmations; and then she became intensely serious as she addressed the group, emphasising yet again the importance of the need to heal the fundamental cause of low self-esteem: she described how its unhealthy energy is carried by many people whose self-perception is marred by being undervalued; she looked strained as she spoke of how individuals may have their confidence completely destroyed by being frequently told they are not good enough; and she talked of the pain people endure as they strive in vain to rise above such untruths and ultimately have their mistaken self-belief apparently confirmed by life-long difficulties which deeply scar their personalities.

She went on to explain how her goal was to help them understand how it is possible to regain self-worth and retain self-respect even when the world around continues to perpetuate the myth of powerlessness.

"And now," she said in a more relaxed tone, "as you have all spontaneously made your way here, would you like us to continue our self-exploration this afternoon?"

"Surely you're not expecting us to believe our presence here is spontaneous?!" chuckled Frank.

"We're beginning to realise you have a subliminal plan for us," grinned Malcolm, "and we love you for it! Let's continue!"

"Indeed," she smiled. "My plan follows your methods of effective teaching and patient nurturing of your children: you aim towards a goal, give praise when it is reached, and thereafter move the goal onward. In the same way I'd like you to take small steps towards the goal of living a life where you totally value yourself; initially you should replace your destructive emotions with an attitude of self-belief, and dismiss your negative thoughts through the use of positive affirmations."

"What on earth do you mean?" Maria interrupted.

"We need some examples," Gabby added.

"Sorry!" Vanessa frowned, "I have a burning desire for you to grasp these things, but then I lose you in the excitement of progress! Let's see: ...replace your destructive emotions with an attitude of self-belief..."

"I've got an example!" exclaimed Laura.

"Go on then, tell us!" Maria replied.

"My destructive emotion is when I think I'm having an awful day; the pain is too much to bear, I cry that I can't face any more...and I just want to..."

"Oh God, Laura, I don't see how it's possible to emerge from such a terrible, terrible thing," whispered Malcolm.

"Oh yes, it's possible; I have a long, private cry, and afterwards I bathe my face; then as I look in the mirror I talk to my reflection..."

"She has a knack of saying such lovely things about herself," interrupted Frank, "her words are like a flowing river of self-love: she talks about her eyes, her skin, the sky above filled with fluffy clouds, her children, her husband, her feet, her hands, her healer, her doctor, the dogs, love, fear, hope, birthdays, her future...then she emerges from the bathroom, ready to receive my hugs of awe and love."

They sat in silence.

"We don't know what to say," Malcolm murmured, "so instead of speaking may I also give you a hug of awe and love?"

"Yes, that includes all of us," said Vanessa, "love, from the depth of our soul."

After some moments of shared thoughts and feelings Vanessa expressed their joint opinion, "Laura, I'm deeply humbled by your courage, strength and self-love. There is really nothing more that needs to be said, or should be said, today."

"I disagree," Laura replied. "I have lots to learn from you so that I may have a better quality of life when I am fully recovered, so please, *please* continue exactly as you planned. You were saying that positive affirmations are small steps, so what is the major lesson for us today? We didn't spontaneously gather here just to hear about my self-belief regime!"

Vanessa gulped, "Laura, you can't imagine how difficult it is for me to describe strategies that are so procedural while you show us the way naturally and with such determination."

"With respect, Vanessa," interrupted Frank, "you have forgotten that Laura has uncovered all these positive qualities directly because of her sessions with you. So please, as she said, continue exactly as planned."

The group spontaneously applauded their resolution and after a short interval resumed their learning circle.

"This is what I was intending to say: Our discussions have focussed upon the matter of self-esteem, but there is something more to be learned; so, while we *all* continue to work upon ourselves as Laura has demonstrated, I would also like to intensely accelerate your spiritual progress by drawing your attention to your spirit self; so, let's return once more to focus upon the energy centred at your heart."

Vanessa paused again; she closed her eyes and placed the palm of her right hand on her heart; instinctively her students copied her action,

"As we do this," she said, "I am reminded of Malcolm's question the other week."

"Who am I?!"

"I am so glad you remembered, Malcolm."

"I remember the distant look in your eyes, Vanessa; your expression revealed your depth; it's where I sense you become more intense and serious."

"Mystical," added Frank.

"That's when we know we need to pay special attention," said Maria.

Vanessa smiled, and then cautiously led them into her thought: "As you have said earlier today, we have a wonderful community here based in our little school, where children are encouraged to what, Malcolm?"

"Value themselves, do their best, respect others."

"They are rewarded for good work and for high achievement," said Laura.

"And encouraged when they are struggling," remarked Colin.

"And told off when they run," said Maria.

"Yes, yes, we are working on educating *all* our staff, really we are," insisted Malcolm with a smile. "And we are convinced that our school philosophy rejects the world's mistaken ethos of competition, fighting to be first, beating others down, demanding rights, or believing we must be good."

"Exactly," nodded Vanessa, "and now our group will be instrumental in leading the community towards the next step."

"Yes," murmured Colin, "the others told me your thought would surpass my written ideas."

"The specific truth is this," she said emphatically. "Everything you accept for yourselves, and thereby teach the children: your best is good enough; be diligent and patient; accept reward for effort as well as success; be helpful and work as a team; strive for excellence... are all vast improvements upon the world of competition and its mistaken belief that it is essential to be 'good' in order to be successful.

However, when you identify yourself as absolutely and totally your spirit self, therein lies the extraordinary certainty: that everything you ever desired of yourself, and for yourself; everything you ever could be, would want to be, or ought to be, *you already are* and *so is everyone else."*

There was another period of silence until the stillness was broken by the sound of their measured, meditative breathing...

Malcolm gazed searchingly at the floor and in a tone which suggested he'd just made a momentous discovery, he whispered, "It's the answer to the question: Who am I?"

"And the answer is: *you are your spirit self,*" cried Gabby. "I get it! If I stop listening to my little self who thinks she is useless, the little me who has been told all her life she is an idiot, and if I be kind to her and tell her she is loved, I will boost my self-esteem so that I won't feel abused by all the father figures in my life. And *then*, as I take notice of my soul, I will realise that I have a lovely light inside which, as you said, is my natural self."

"Beautifully said, though the immense truth that you will all eventually come to realise is this: not only do you *have* a lovely light inside, but, in fact, you *are* that light; you are *totally, wholly light,*" Vanessa finished, boldly.

Yet another natural pause in their deliberations enabled them to be comfortably silent as they each felt a profound sense of inner contentment.

Once more Malcolm interrupted their stillness, "So, to return to my earlier conversation with Colin, Laura and Sophie," he probed, "we have a good school ethos which goes beyond society's expectation of striving and competition; we endorse self-respect, effort, team spirit and praise, but now we desire our children to know that there is a reality beyond these aspirations which affirms that they are intrinsically 'perfect.'

My new questions are these: How do we teach this? And if we succeed with our teaching, will we not collapse into a smug state of bliss where we don't care and where we actually demotivate ourselves and our children with the assertion that we are already light, so we don't really need to bother?"

"That really wouldn't happen, would it?" interrupted Colin. "We could not love ourself and be satisfied solely with a sense of personal bliss, nor could we love ourself and not care, because when we truly love ourself by responding to our spirit, those kinds of behaviour would be impossible."

"Absolutely!" added Laura. "And the knowledge that we are intrinsically all that we would ever want to be surely means that we appreciate ourself without even *trying*, because we will have discovered what it is to be our natural self."

"So, we get out of bed knowing we are all goodness, and when things happen that are good or bad, we just keep stepping along knowing we're on the way to complete ourself," murmured Gabby.

"That is an excellent phrase!" said Vanessa. "We're on a journey to complete ourself!"

"But what does it mean?" asked Maria.

"Throughout the journey of life we express ourselves with thoughts and emotions through our body; at some point we discover our all-knowing soul which has been constantly functioning in the background of our existence; when we realise the significance of our soul and allow it to be freely expressed, it interacts and combines with mind and body so that we feel 'whole'."

"As we talk, I get a hint of it," murmured Sophie. "It's so calming; I feel self-assured because I sense my inner self is constantly awake and aware; it makes me feel that I do not need anyone else to make me feel happy, content..."

"...or good," added Gabby.

"Me too!" exclaimed Laura. "As I come close to that feeling I realise that I am not dependent upon anything outside of me because *I* am in control of me."

"And it *does* begin with me," breathed Malcolm. "I must teach *me* before I teach others; I need to meditate and keep repeating: 'Who am I' in order to react as my spirit self and discover true self-assurance."

Vanessa smiled as she summed up their revelation: "You are well on the way to creating a wondrous learning environment. All spiritual wisdom begins with acknowledging oneself in ways which you, the Sputnik group, will continue to discover. It will be a lifelong task. Your skill as educators and parents is to create ways of nudging yourselves towards paying attention to your inner self every day.

True self belief is a state of heart and mind where you totally respond to your spirit's assurance that you already are itself; this realisation awakens wisdom, and then wisdom adjusts perception; this means that every day you step out knowing that, at heart, you already are your perfect self, and with that knowledge you create aims for your everyday life in order to reach the ultimate goal of complete self-awareness; your wisdom brings peace, patience and endurance for each small step of your learning journey."

"You've set us some difficult homework!" said Colin.

"Indeed I have! And now we have time for a cup of tea and an opportunity to reflect before some of you leave to collect your children."

After they had gone, Malcolm remained to share his concern with Vanessa,

"You know, I believe what you say, and I can see by how you live – giving precedence to your spirit self – that your life is enriched; indeed, from what you have previously told me about your own struggles, this practice has helped you live through immense challenges. What concerns me is how to remember and use all that you teach us; when you close your eyes and speak as spirit I'm afraid I won't understand."

"Your concerns show how much you care, Malcolm. I know you care about your family and the children in your school, and your continued struggles during our meetings show you are learning to care for yourself too. Have no fear; all that we discuss in Sputnik's Hub is being integrated into your psyche, like warmth seeping into your bones. The miracle of this is that you do not need to understand it all, just trust yourself enough to allow the wisdom to permeate your being.

You believe you are learning something new, but in fact I am simply helping you all to remember what the world has caused you to forget; this is a re-awakening where you will uncover and become your true self in all its power and glory."

"And this will happen for me one day? How will I find myself?"

"Dear Malcolm, when I speak of 'becoming' your true self, I mean that you naturally 'change state'; this means that you no longer live simply as your material or worldly self, instead you recognise yourself as spirit, and as such you naturally find contentment – whatever choices you make through life."

Malcolm relaxed into their conversation: "Tell me, Vanessa, this question that is so important to you..."

"Who Am I?"

"Yes. Why does it interest me so much?"

She smiled. "It's a saying, a mantra, which has been recommended by gurus through the ages, and it delights me that you have latched onto its significance; it's not meant to be answered, and it's not a rhetorical question either; indeed, when you keep 'Who am I' in your thought - especially when you go to sleep, and upon waking - it has the effect of reminding you not to sabotage yourself with negative self-perception."

Malcolm frowned as she continued, "For example, when you are concerned with Stevie, you understand that he is a bright little soul who is weighed down by circumstances, and as you find ways to support and help him you know you can't simply offer him the mantra 'Who Am I', though it is possible for you to instruct him about this in ways that he can understand; and ultimately the resolution of his difficulties will reveal wisdom for you too."

"A little child leading?" he grinned.

"Well, it would do us all good to be more childlike – not childish though!" She looked at the head-teacher sternly. "The real Stevie is not his angry self in the classroom, nor his struggling self with a reading book; it is not his reactive self with other children, nor his cheeky self with his siblings."

"I get it," Malcolm interrupted, "I see a little boy trying to emerge from a cocoon of bewilderment, a bright little spark trying to make sense of his predicament."

"You see his light within, you recognise his natural self, despite what others think of him."

"And I fear he'll gradually get worse when he finds himself accepting what others say about him."

"Unless you step in and offer an environment which allows the children to break away from validating untruths such as, a bad boy, a difficult child and a misfit, and help them to understand that no-one is defined by their thoughts, emotions or behaviour."

"How do I do that? Your ideas go way beyond my positive school ethos; how do I create an even better place for our children to work and live?"

"Ask yourself, 'Who Am I?' and keep asking, over and over again, repeat it to yourself so that the phrase becomes self-watch-words."

"Vanessa?"

"Umm?"

"You do know that I love you?"

"Yes, Malcolm, I know," she murmured.

Chapter 9   Sacred Space

"Come in. I was expecting you." Vanessa's welcome stunned Sophie's husband as he hesitated on her doorstep.

For some time he had struggled with his decision to meet the woman whose presence had clearly benefitted his wife and children, and as he made his way to Vanessa's home he re-examined his dilemma.

He revelled in the renewed feeling of what he supposed was "joy" which had recently transformed his home into a comforting and stimulating place, just as it had been in the early days of his marriage; however, he clung to his own firmly grounded and practical ideas which focussed upon the material aspects of life, giving no credence to anything ethereal; he thought that any eccentricity ought to be avoided, and his gut feeling led him to the conclusion that he should keep well away from the strange person in their village.

Yet, having firmly made this decision, his mind persisted in re-examining his difficulty; he could not doubt that Vanessa's influence upon his wife had changed the atmosphere in his home for the better, and even though he now looked forward to returning to Sophie each evening, he continued to experience a sense of domestic dis-ease which unnerved him. He wondered whether, like Sophie, he needed emotional and psychological help, though he strongly resisted the idea of revealing his anxiety to another man, albeit a medical professional, and so after much deliberation he finally decided to find the woman in whom his wife had placed so much confidence.

He reasoned that he could not turn up at "Sputnik's Hub" with the excuse that he considered its philosophy to be idealistic nonsense and the crowded room personally intimidating, so he planned to find its instigator in her own home in order to gain some sense of what she was really like.

As he approached Vanessa's cottage he was surprised how ordinary it seemed, and he smiled to himself at the ridiculous notion that he had probably been anticipating some kind of witch's coven. On the contrary, he was quite charmed by the quaint footbridge which gave access to Vanessa's home on the opposite side of the river, though upon arrival at her door he was troubled by her greeting:

"Expecting me? Has my wife been talking about me?"

"Your wife? You mean Sophie? No, she has not spoken of you; nonetheless it's never long before a caring husband comes to seek out the person who has been influencing the one he loves. After all, you do care, don't you? It's natural that you would want to be satisfied that your wife is safe with me," Vanessa smiled.

He immediately warmed to her and settled easily into a chair in her living room. He thought it bizarre to be so quickly drinking tea, and was amazed that he could immediately talk about his most intimate and sensitive concerns.

"I'm so afraid. I love my wife, I'm sure I do, but..." he stammered.

"Intimacy is a state of mind, not a state of heart," she murmured. "Are you able to talk to me about your mother?"

Confused and disturbed by Vanessa's directness, he exclaimed, "My mother? What can she have to do with this?"

"Well, it is likely that a man who experiences difficulties in being sexually intimate with his wife may need to evaluate the way his mother behaves towards him."

Still feeling somewhat stunned by Vanessa's candidness, he nevertheless began to feel safe in her compassion, and immediately understood why Sophie felt drawn to her. He loosened his tie, unbuttoned his collar, leaned back in the chair and closed his eyes.

"I call my mother, Chief, because that's what she is, she's the boss. Whatever mother says has to be accepted. She is forceful, and I am sure she has a heart of gold somewhere hidden behind her granite exterior."

"What about her relationship with your father?"

"As I said, she's the boss. Dad would never dream of contradicting her; he is extremely placid, and really just wants a quiet life."

"Is it your sense that your mother may have a higher regard for you than for your father?"

"Well, in a practical sense, yes. I know how to get things done; I'm a go-getter, something that I imagine she likes; whereas my dad lets life float along. Some might envy his relaxed way of living because nothing ever seems to bother him, but I like to have a definite purpose in my life, even a sense of adventure."

"I imagine your mother likes that about you; perhaps she values your adventurous spirit and would like to be a partner with you in some projects?"

"Maybe. I'm not sure. She's never said so. Actually, she and Dad are very close, they're always together; in fact, she has him follow wherever she leads, even holding hands...at their age!"

"I am sure they love each other very much," Vanessa replied. "However, there is a part of every female which prefers not to be in control; in fact, the core of the feminine, though it is powerful, actually desires to be led, cared for and directed. This need comes from the fundamental nature of the relationship of the feminine with the masculine; I'd like to express this in spiritual terms: feminine energy flows freely like an eternal river, but in order to create from her expanse, she needs structure, and it is masculine energy which satisfies this need."

"Somehow, I understand what you mean," he said, though he frowned in bewilderment.

"I would guess that your 'Chief' naturally enjoys your nick-name for her? But tell me, how is her relationship with Sophie?"

"Ah, that's the thing. They don't relate – at all. Sophie and she have never got on, and I can't understand what happens between them; it's like some kind of secret battle. They have never openly argued, but they speak about each other as if they had."

"They may be experiencing a clandestine fight over one man."

"What? Who? Sophie would never fight with anyone, though Mother...well, she likes to be the chief. Sophie puts up with a lot so that our children get to see their grandparents; it often makes her irritable and angry and we do tend to fall out about it. Look, I'm afraid I don't understand what you are saying, are you inferring that Sophie is in some way resisting my desire for her and somehow making it so that I cannot 'do it' with her?"

"That's not the way I think we should approach this," Vanessa said in a matter-of-fact manner. "I don't think there are any consciously unpleasant motives being used here by Sophie or your mother; let's pause and gain insight into your difficulty."

She smiled and briefly touched his hand, and after taking some deep breaths she closed her eyes and in a measured soft voice she explained, "Each expression of the feminine needs the masculine. Your mother behaves as though she is a fighter and in control, but as an aspect of feminine she has a desire to soften; she has a need to be directed and ultimately to receive guidance or structure from the masculine. She has chosen a husband – your father – who does not offer the whole package of masculine however much they love and care for each other, and subconsciously she sees a strong masculine structure in you. Subconsciously you feel her need, so there is an aspect of your masculine which is pulled with a sense of responsibility towards her."

"What? No, that cannot be right," he responded indignantly.

Gently Vanessa continued, "This does not mean there is a sexual desire between you and your mother, but I am suggesting that there is a subconscious feminine control from her which affects you in realms that are difficult to acknowledge, and as a result there is created deep within you an inexplicable guilt about enjoying sexual intimacy with Sophie. Hence, you can no longer 'do it' as you say - especially now that you have produced the children you both desperately wanted and needed."

His sharp intake of breath helped to suppress his incredulous anger; Vanessa continued to breathe gently and evenly, and as she opened her eyes her gaze seemed to dissipate his emotion so that he relaxed.

She continued in a firm but gentle tone, "It's not my intention to hurt you, nor insult you and your family, and if you are willing we may continue with a particular healing procedure which will, in my experience, resolve your difficulty on many of life's planes; the process will not harm you, Sophie or your parents, and afterwards, when you feel its effect, you will understand its process; though if you are uncertain about continuing we can simply finish by sharing tea together. Alternatively, you may like to go away and think about what we have discussed and return another day."

"I have to follow my gut," he said slowly, "and right now I feel really peaceful, so if you don't mind I'd like us to continue."

She nodded. "First, may I suggest you take a comfort break?"

He smiled, "Please, I'm bursting; must be all that tea!"

As he returned to the living room he commented: "You have a really nice home; it feels...special, though it's not what I imagined."

"You expected incense and buddhas, jangling beads and prayer flags."

He grinned.

"I have those...if you'd like," she said mischievously, "but I find there is spirituality in everything, even in the trappings of a 'really nice home'. The specialness you feel here is perfect love – the kind that surpasses understanding; it permeates my home because everything here – the material of the dwelling and the people within it – know that they are loved. Now, are you sure you are comfortable? May we begin?"

They resumed their seats and with eyes closed breathed deeply in surprising synchronicity.

Vanessa's voice sounded commanding, "As we have discussed, my home is safe, suffused with love and perfectly balanced to enable us to work for 'highest good'."

"It's a sacred space," he murmured, hardly believing he could offer such a description.

"Sacred; no longer scared?" she opened an eye to share the moment with him.

He smiled and nodded, then settled as if dozing in his armchair.

"You may feel sleepy, though this procedure is nothing like hypnosis," she continued, "in fact you are very much awake to the conscious depth of this session; and as you settle, we invite the consciousness of members of your family to join us, though as we have affirmed, our work is entirely for you with its agenda determined by our earlier conversation."

Again, he nodded.

Vanessa proceeded to talk throughout the session as if she was giving a descriptive commentary of events as they unfolded:

"Your mother is here, standing in front of you, though you should understand that the image I see epitomizes the spiritual consciousness of your mother; she appears accompanied by two babies whom she holds tenderly. They are the spirit bodies of the two infants Sophie 'lost' at birth; the two babies who were 'still born'. Your mother has appeared with them and continues to hold on to them because she chooses to do so; in her heart she considers herself to be matriarch, and in maintaining this position she has taken a subconscious, one might say etheric, responsibility for her first two grandchildren. Now she comes towards you because she wants to bring the children to you. Do you wish to receive them?"

"I'm not sure," he stammered, "Sophie ought to be the one to hold them again; I remember the look in her eyes as she held their little bodies... Still can't believe this happened to her - to us - twice..." he choked.

"You are perfectly in touch with wisdom," Vanessa whispered tenderly, "and in fact, over to your left is the spirit consciousness of Sophie; she moves to be close beside you."

Vanessa paused in her description to comment upon the evolving image:

"You have wonderfully placed yourself at the spiritual meeting of your mother and your wife; and as usual in spiritual realms, when people are brought together with heart-filled agenda their everyday difficulties are set aside to fulfil the desires of their soul."

Her commentary continued: "Your mother draws near to hand the babies across your open lap so that she may gift them back to Sophie through you."

Tears squeezed through his closed eyes as he welcomed the spirits of his first two children with open palms ready to receive and give.

"And now," she went on, "Sophie shows how very capable she is as a mother; she gathers both her babies into her arms and draws them to her breasts; eagerly they accept her maternal food because in some respects they are in need of sustenance."

Vanessa opened her eyes and paused to allow the young father to have time to absorb the emotion of the moment.

After a while, in a firmer tone she said, "As the babies remain with their mother for this instant in eternity, we invite the consciousness of all three to leave our session, knowing that there needs to be further spiritual work accomplished with them, and I will see that this is done.

However, we now turn our attention to the other mother here with us; indeed, we thank her for bringing her first grandchildren to us and for caring for them spiritually. Nonetheless, we affirm that it is now time for grandma to be relieved and cleansed of the consciousness of the little ones so that she is free from carrying this spiritual burden."

Vanessa moved her hand in front of her as if sweeping matter aside.

"Having offered cleansing to your mother, we turn our attention to the consciousness of your father who stands nearby, somewhat behind your mother."

They smiled recognising the symbolism of the dynamics of the relationship between husband and wife.

Vanessa's voice became more commanding:

"Speaking to you, parents of the young man receiving healing here. Your son, following our earlier deliberations, wishes to affirm a healthy relationship with each of you: Son to Father,"

Vanessa directed her arm from the embodied son to the consciousness of his father.

"Son to Mother," she repeated her movements.

"And my healing role is to sever any other connections that may exist between you." She performed actions with her hand as if slicing through the air, and then coughed to indicate that the disconnection was complete.

While pausing to check his reaction she gently placed her hand on the young man's shoulder, and then she explained:

"This energetic process has confirmed that from now on the relationship between you and each of your parents will be healthy and well-balanced. You will begin to notice a subtle difference in your day to day relationship with your mother and father, and Sophie will feel more comfortable with your mother. How this plays out in your intimacy with your wife...well, you will see," she smiled.

"Now, tell me," she said, gently, "How do you feel?"

"Sort of relieved," he whispered, "Can you tell me, will my mother be all right?"

"She will, as we conclude the session," Vanessa assured him.

With a strong voice she declared: "I invite Mother and Father to join in their mutual love and respectful union, and as they embrace, I request light from above to shine over them, through them and around them, and as this healthy union is confirmed I request that their spirit consciousness returns completely and totally to their conscious selves.

And so it is."

"That was beautiful," he breathed. "It was incredible; as you were speaking I saw a vision of my parents standing together wrapped in a beautiful hug; their expression suggested they were enjoying being bathed in a glorious spotlight – I guess some would say they merged in a beacon of God's light, though I don't know about such things..."

He remained quiet and still while Vanessa waited and watched as his glowing expression gradually relaxed into a contented smile. After a while he opened his eyes, wiped his cheeks and nervously straightened his tie, and then, clearing his throat, he shifted himself awkwardly in his chair.

"Drink all of this water," Vanessa encouraged him, "it's necessary to help cleanse your body after the healing."

He accepted the drink without speaking and seemingly embarrassed and overwhelmed he got up and hastily moved towards the door.

"You need time to yourself," Vanessa advised, "I recommend a walk in the wind and sunshine; just give yourself time to be, and when you feel you'd like some explanation, you know where to find me!"

"I do, indeed. I'd like to visit you again, Vanessa; though right now I'm overwhelmed and in a state of, well...awe." He fumbled an attempt to hug her, and resorted to a perfunctory hand shake. "You know... you're amazing," he paused and bit his lip, "really amazing...but, rest assured, I'll never discuss this with anyone."

Wistfully she watched as he walked back towards the village along the riverside path, and when he finally disappeared from sight, she firmly closed her door.

Chapter 10   Moving Images

Lunch times had become popular at Sputnik's Hub as Maria successfully learned to present healthy and tasty dishes; occasionally Stevie was allowed to choose a friend to accompany him to help set tables and comment on the menu. The venue had gained a reputation in the community as a place for value meals and relaxed conversation, and Colin was particularly delighted to have instigated a formal monthly "Lunch 'n lecture" which had begun to attract experts on a variety of metaphysical topics who presented talks to an audience growing in number and enthusiasm.

However, the original Sputnik group made sure that their own precious time together for discussion, learning and support remained sacrosanct: whilst having confidence in the aims of the whole organisation, they agreed that their group sessions were of immense importance for their well-being especially when they carefully planned an agenda which enabled them to prepare and look forward to a time of intense communion with Vanessa.

It was unusual for them to arrange a meeting without knowing who might be the focus of their collective thought, but as they gathered for what seemed to be an impromptu get-together they quickly had no doubt that Frank was in immediate need of their support and love.

He arrived looking tired and distracted: his complexion was grey and drawn and his hair unusually dishevelled; his usual habit of greeting them individually to give each his personal attention was overlooked, and instead he walked past the waiting group to lean heavily against the kitchen counter; after a few moments of hesitation he stumbled back into the main room; nervously he pushed his fingers through his hair and slumped heavily into his chair, "It's Laura," he mumbled, "it's bad news, it's very bad news."

The friends exchanged concerned glances in stunned silence.

Gabby was first to attempt to ease the tension, "Talk to us, Frank," she murmured, as she placed her arm across his shoulders; "talking isn't everything, but it's a start and it'll help us understand how we may help you."

"I never thought this would happen to me - to us," he whispered. "It's true we had been expecting it, in fact, dreading the confirmation of what we already knew."

He continued as though talking to himself, "The times I've heard that phrase...many times I've attended accidents and incidents, and it's the first remark people make: 'I never thought this would happen to me.' Why do you think we say it?"

His preoccupied state suggested he was not looking for an explanation, but Colin clearly wanted to help, "It's human self-protection," he remarked, sadly. "If we lived in anticipation of such things we'd never cope, and if we had an inkling of tragedy and grief we wouldn't be able to face our tomorrows."

"Anyhow," interrupted Maria, briskly, "we're all gonna 'elp you cope. It's usually you 'elping me, remember?" She sounded as though she was talking with Stevie, persuading him to go into class, and as she hugged Frank she assured him, "Now I'm gonna do my very best for you and Laura – in *every* way I can."

"What are Vanessa's thoughts?" Malcolm asked, quietly.

"Laura and I spent a long time with her the other day; our children were there too... and while we were there I thought I was handling the situation quite well, but today something inside me wants to burst... can't find the wherewithal to be mature and competent... I've come here for help... please help... want to explode... it always feels safe here... I don't know what to do..."

"We created this place together," murmured Colin. "It's filled with love, compassion and wisdom, and you are one of the founding stalwarts, but today it is perfectly fine for you to cry and allow us to support you."

"I thought I'd be able to use what we've learned about power and wisdom instead of collapsing like a helpless little boy."

"First you need to be vulnerable and allow your emotion to pour out; let your tears clear away your fear and stress," murmured Gabby.

"And then your big strong heart will open like the Frank we know and love," said Maria, still sounding as though she was giving encouragement to her youngest son.

"And you'll find your spirit self," declared Colin.

"Yes, your natural self," Gabby concluded. "Then, whatever the future holds, you will be able to react wisely and peacefully."

Malcolm leapt to his feet and paced the room, "You all sound like self-righteous prigs," he shouted, angrily. "We're only just learning this stuff and we're behaving as though we can smooth Frank's terror away with a bunch of wise thoughts.

I can't bear to see you like this, Frank, I really can't; it's just not *fair*."

"Calm down, calm down," said Colin, firmly. "Obviously we're all shocked and upset; our comments are just panicky responses to Laura's enormous challenge.

Now Frank, if you feel able, please do what Malcolm suggested - prior to his outburst – and tell us how Vanessa approached this so that we can somehow find the best way to combine our thoughts with her work."

Frank relaxed as he described the session with Vanessa, "As I said, we went together as a family, but she addressed us separately:

For Laura, she told her to think about the sea, especially the waves of the sea flowing in and out, breaking on the shore and retreating... forward and back...

She asked her to recall the *sound* each wave makes as it breaks and retreats against a pebbled beach, inward and out... forward and back...

She reminded Laura that the ocean waves continue to break and retreat even when we as summer visitors leave the coast behind: forever and ever breaking and retreating, forward and back... in and out...

I recall now how Vanessa particularly emphasised what is really an obvious situation: when we're at the shore we watch the movement of the waves, sometimes becoming mesmerised by their rhythm, and of course, the action continues even when we are no longer there to observe the tide; then, whenever we return to the shoreline we can be certain that the waves will be there, breaking and retreating, as if we'd never been away.

When I think about this I want to cry. What do you suppose she wanted Laura to understand?"

"Well, her relaxing image makes me think of the constancy of everlasting peace, the eternal flow of love which is unfailing and always available to us even when we're not aware of its presence; it's constantly there, relentless and tireless, but life's troubles tend to make us feel disconnected from its comfort," said Sophie pensively. "Now where did that thought come from? It's not something I would normally say, is it?"

"You've responded while you're in a tranquil, meditative state and so you're able to access profound wisdom," said Colin, confidently. "You know, picturing that ocean scene makes me feel incredibly calm and peaceful; and Frank, you also seem to be gradually regaining your usual composure; am I right?"

Frank hardly noticed the interruption; he seemed intent on recalling every moment of the time his family had shared with Vanessa:

"So, Laura's homework was to meditate upon waves at the shore.

For me, Vanessa had a similar image really. She described bamboo stalks bending in the wind; bending, yet righting themselves... bending almost over, and then blowing back to be perfectly upright; as she spoke I imagined that I could hear the swish of the wind amongst the stalks and leaves.

I'm reminded that bamboo stalks are strong but they still have the capacity to bend almost flat to the ground without breaking, and they have a natural ability to right themselves when the wind subsides.

You know," he seemed to emerge from his altered state, "I'm going to plant bamboo near the house; it will remind me that strength is not about having the power to resist, but it is the ability to accept the consequences of a great challenge, and to be patient and endure until the precise moment when natural power exerts itself to bring back normality."

"We should create a planted area around Sputnik's Hub," said Colin. "Bamboo will be our first item, and then we will all be reminded that there is intrinsic strength in a will which may, through adverse circumstances, be forced to the ground. It should make us all feel, well...*empowered*."

"Umm," Frank murmured, still barely aware of his audience, his mind was absorbed in Vanessa's wisdom:

"For the children, she made them wait in anticipation as she delved into a paper bag and brought out flower bulbs, one for each of them. Laura and I watched and listened as she talked; it seemed as though we were being taken back into her classroom to see how she used to work with young children many years ago!

She was as engrossed as the children as she asked them to feel their bulb's rough, loose outer layers; then she encouraged them to hold the bulb in the palm of their hand and imagine life energy pulsating through it. She explained how even though the external skin of the bulb is dry and crusty it provides good protection for its inner smooth lushness; then she talked about how life inside is held back until the bulb is planted and cared for.

She gave them paper and coloured pencils and asked them to draw how their bulb would be after planting - when its shoot and roots emerge, when it buds and flowers, and when it loses its bloom and withers.

While they were busy with their art, Laura and I sobbed and held each other; we were thinking how the bulb's life cycle is like our own...and of course we are both very emotional about such things at the moment, but I'm still not sure why Vanessa brought flower bulbs to our attention; perhaps she wanted the children to understand the cycle of life, death and life again, but I wonder, did she deliberately want to stir our emotions? Because really, she didn't need a powerful image to bring us to tears...me and Laura are already expert at crying," he shook his head, miserably.

"I know how it feels to be in the midst of great sadness and have such terrible pain inside," murmured Sophie, "so I can appreciate a little of what you're going through. But strangely, as you spoke, I experienced something quite beautiful; you've touched such powerful emotion and I feel as though the love you share with Laura has caused something significant to happen within me, I actually felt a change inside me, as though my heart moved. I know this is about your suffering, Frank, but you have aroused a shared grief, and somehow made it better."

He smiled distantly, but again continued as if he hadn't really heard his friend's reaction:

"Then we had a period of quiet while Vanessa placed her hands on parts of our body, not just Laura's, but mine and the kids' too; she sort of hummed - toned she called it – and when she touched my forehead it felt cool and calming, though her hand against my skin was warm; when she placed her palms on my shoulders it felt as if an enormous weight had lifted from me; her hands kept returning to rest against my heart, and then she touched my hands, my knees and my feet.

I have no idea why she selected those parts of me, but it was obvious why her gentle touch lingered over Laura's breasts and tummy. I desperately pray that the healing will do some good, but I'm so afraid that my doubts will make any possible miracle fail.

The kids were rather subdued; they patiently accepted Vanessa's touch and surprisingly didn't even raise a torrent of questions which normally happens when they discover something new; and later at home they busied themselves planting the bulbs; you know how children are – despite their concern for their mother, when they are outside playing, mercifully they are able to forget their sadness.

And Laura... you know, she has such strength and determination, I've no idea where it comes from; even when she's in considerable pain she manages to look serene; she says she is constantly accompanied by loving thought which keeps her going; and me... look at me, I've withered and collapsed at a time when I need to be strong, and I'm just not used to being so weak."

"Not weak, Frank," Vanessa spoke from the doorway.

Even though she was expected, the quietness of her approach caused them to start in surprise; it seemed to the group that she always found the most poignant moment to arrive, primed with an uncanny ability to calm heightened emotions.

Chapter 11   Seed of Hope

As Vanessa entered, the atmosphere seemed to change as if the room had suddenly transformed into a peaceful spiritual sanctuary, and in the eyes of the hushed group she appeared to almost glide over the polished floor towards them; instinctively and expectantly they settled into their familiar chairs.

Vanessa held her hands against her body: her right hand protected the enclosed palm of her left in which she carefully carried a few tiny seeds; she moved around the group and placed just one seed on the outstretched palm of each of them.

"This seems like religious ceremony," remarked Gabby.

"Perhaps, though I would like this to be a spiritual affirmation rather than a ritual," Vanessa replied as she firmly placed a seed in Frank's trembling hand.

Her touch affected him deeply, "I don't know how to behave as we all hoped we might when faced with life's challenges," he murmured. "Our meetings now seem only idle talk about good intentions. I need to find myself. How do I do that? I had such fine words to offer others a few weeks ago; what were they? How do I remember them for myself? How do I live the way we intended?"

"Ah, yes, how to walk our talk," Vanessa sighed. "It's never easy. Even after years of practice we tend to stumble and fail."

"What? Even you?"

"Especially me," she replied. "But the task – and the joy – is to constantly find ways to remember…"

"…our light inside?" Gabby suggested.

Vanessa nodded and then went on to explain why she had brought her handful of gifts: "I've offered each of you a tiny seed to stimulate your thinking heart; let's spend some time in contemplation with nature's creative power in mind…"

The group became silent as they each examined the small speck in their hand, and then like inquisitive children their chatter erupted,

"I've never seriously thought how such a little thing can grow into a plant, a flower or even a tree; it's so tiny, dry and hard," exclaimed Gabby.

"Yes, and just think, if I planted this in a pot and put it on my kitchen window sill, and if I made sure I watered and cared for it, I'd soon have a beautiful flower…from Vanessa. I'n't that just perfect?" Maria whispered, in childlike awe.

"It is indeed totally amazing," said Vanessa, "and I hope you will use this moment to remember that you too, all of you, are totally amazing." She paused to emphasise her point. "It's so very important that you realise how wonderful you are; and just as seeds are planted, watered and nurtured to enable their essence to break free and grow, so you must nurture yourselves, pay attention to who you are, and allow your natural self to break free from the crusty restriction of your negative feelings, destructive thoughts and low self-image."

The circle of friends resumed their contemplation of the seeds and continued to share their inspired thought:

"If we could crack open the tiny seed, there'd be nothing to see inside," Sophie mused.

"And that is precisely the amazing wonder which I also want you to realise," said Vanessa, seriously. "The great and powerful that makes things grow is imperceptible; it is life, life-giving and living."

"I just need to think about Sophie's comment," said Colin, excitedly. "I can't believe through all my years as an educator I've never contemplated the inside of a seed and realised that actually there is nothing there!"

"Yes. And the nothing becomes something when it is cherished," said Gabby.

"But the 'nothing' really must be 'something'... something big and amazing for it to be life-giving," added Malcolm, thoughtfully. "Though it's not actually 'nothing'; what's inside is simply undetectable."

"No... thing," whispered Frank, as though mesmerised. "Ah! Vanessa, you're teaching us about the power of 'no thing': this absolute wonder of the universe is 'no thing'; it can't ever be an ordinary 'thing' because it is far greater than anything we can possibly imagine, and yet it is in everything."

"Indeed, dear Frank; and furthermore, it *is* everything. As I said: it is *life, life-giving and living.*"

Frank began to sob profusely, and his friends quietly waited allowing him to express his emotion freely: during their time together they had learned of the necessity for each of them to periodically shed tears, safe in the knowledge that no-one amongst them would say, "Please don't cry."

Eventually Malcolm whispered, "Vanessa, I'm beginning to have a clearer understanding of your method of teaching, guiding and leading us: initially, I thought your imaginative stories materialised just because you are obviously an excellent teacher, but now I think there is an inexplicable power which comes through your images. Am I correct?"

Vanessa leaned back in her chair and closed her eyes, "Images are the language of the soul," she sighed serenely. "My pictures, stories and tokens will remain with you forever, and when each 'spring to mind' your thought will grasp the wisdom of your soul and bring its truth forward to actively work with your emotional self and your physical being."

"A case of mind influencing matter, then?" suggested Colin.

"Well, not quite," Vanessa paused reflectively, "you will recall that we've previously discussed a little about the power and influence of the mind over the body."

"I remember that day *very* well," Gabby interrupted. "I learned then that when my mind is in control my daily events tend to unravel like an unruly spring."

"But there are positive outcomes of mind over matter," Colin persisted.

"Without a doubt," Vanessa agreed, "the relationship between the mind and body is strong, as is the relationship between the body and our emotions; indeed, the body, emotions and mind are an ascending order of vibrational energy throughout our being, and when all are working for the self, then mind over matter works to good effect.

However, the relationship between body and mind needs conscious work and diligent effort to be effective, and it is always influenced by motive; what I mean is: the mind has a habit of going astray – off upon its own mission, so to speak - and frequently it is mistaken about what is best for the whole person; whereas when spirit is called upon, it naturally works for 'highest good'. In fact, when spirit's purpose is realised by each individual, the process of its interaction with the mind and body becomes perfectly natural rather than a hard-working effort of mind over matter."

"I think I need another picture to help me understand," Gabby frowned.

Vanessa paused, "Let's see if this image helps:

Close your eyes and focus upon your gentle breathing; now, imagine a hot, dusty country scene where there's a constant challenge to cultivate sandy soil; life here each day is a battle, trying to scratch a crop from earth's surface. Sometimes the soil accommodates the seed and there is a successful crop, but often soil and seed are incompatible and more work must be done for a successful harvest.

This is a symbol of the daily battle of the mind and emotions struggling to steer their person through life's challenges; metaphorically speaking they are trying to make sense of the heat, the sun and the poor soil whilst hoping for a sprinkling of moisture; it is constant trial and effort with some success especially if the mind happens upon a rain storm of positive thought.

However, imagine in this scene, deep below earth's surface, there is a well-spring of goodness, an ever-flowing supply of life-giving wisdom and guidance..."

"But there has to be a way to access the watery wisdom deep down in such a well," murmured Gabby.

"A rope and a bucket would work," suggested Colin, testily.

"A life-line!" breathed Malcolm. "Your way of using images and poignant ideas is a life-line into the deep well of the soul! You suggest a pictorial image and, like a rope with a bucket, we plumb the depths of spirit's wisdom until eventually we grasp the ideas and draw them up into our psyche."

"Clever choice of words!" said Colin.

"So," said Maria, slowly, "we're tryin' to listen to our own spirit, but Vanessa's stories do the job for us while we're still learnin' about ourselves; her words easily lead us into the world of our soul so that we can use the wisest ideas instead of wonderin' if our mind and emotions are doing the best for us."

"Yes," Vanessa replied, "but actually you may well find that as you practice giving precedence to your spirit, you too will be open to seemingly childlike ideas and images which will stimulate your natural instinct to work with inner wisdom; for example, in everyday life you may suddenly find that song lyrics or catch-phrases will inspire your thinking and 'do the job' - as you put it - of helping you to be consciously in touch with your soul.

In fact, it's really marvellous how the soul expertly attracts your attention once you have metaphorically opened the door to spirit."

In deep thought she gazed ahead and murmured reflectively, "Indeed, images are the language of the soul."

Gabby's inquisitive chatter interrupted the moment of stillness, "Vanessa, I'm grateful for your imaginative explanations, they really do help me grasp the ideas which I find so very difficult, so now will you please explain the unusual phrase which you used a few moments ago?"

They were taken aback by Vanessa's uncharacteristic giggle, "I wondered when someone would ask me to explain: an ascending order of vibrational energy!"

"That's the phrase! What does it mean?"

"Well, on that eventful day which you well remember, Gabby - while we awaited your arrival - I briefly talked about the body's energy centres..."

"The chakras," interrupted Colin, boldly. "After you talked about them I researched the topic and discovered that chakras were studied as long ago as 1500 BC in ancient India; sages at that time described them in their scripture, the *Vedas*."

"Not some New Age mumbo-jumbo then?" said Gabby, slyly.

"Did I say that?"

"You did. When you, Maria and Sophie were explaining what I had missed that day."

"Well, err, I've discovered that the ideas are far from new...in fact, pre-date Christianity, Islam and Buddhism. Do any of you know that Hinduism was practised long before the other major religions?"

"Really," Maria sighed. "What are we doin' talkin' about this stuff when we were goin' to learn somethin' *useful*."

"Alright, you tell us how useful the chakras are!" chided Colin.

"Can I?" Maria asked, glancing towards Vanessa.

"I think you should," said Vanessa, dotingly, "the others ought to know how much time you've given to exploring the art of healing since you worked with Colin's dog."

With an air of importance Maria straightened her back and cleared her throat,

"I'm not good at explainin' but I'll try: When I'm thinkin' about healin', and I look at a person's body, I see colours of the rainbow: red around the bottom, orange near their belly, yellow in the middle, lots of bright green around the heart, some blues near people's neck and face and sometimes purple and white around the top of their head."

"And do the colours mean something?" asked Colin.

"Yes! It's science…I think physics or sumthin'; they say that colour and sound are the way healers see energy; some healers talk about colour when they work and some do their work with sound, so sumtimes they hum or tone while they move their hands over a person's body. And when Vanessa said…err…"

"…ascending order of vibrational energy."

"Yes, that's it; she means that when we start at the bottom of the list of chakras we begin with the one that 'elps a healer work with the physical body; it looks and sounds like red; I mean its energy vibrates the same as the colour red. Then above the body chakra there's the one that's connected to our feelin's; this one looks and sounds like orange; in physics it has a vibration of orange. The chakra above the one about feelin's has energy the same as yellow; and then there's the heart chakra which is higher still and sings like green, and above them all is the chakra of our spirit which feels like blue.

You know, I've bin thinkin' about what Vanessa said just now about going *down* into a pretend well to find our wise self, but when I want to find the way to my spirit I look *upwards* – to the place near my heart and forehead; so p'raps we should look *inside* and *outside*, and *up* and *down*, because our spirit is all around us!"

"What is she talking about?"

"She's describing the sympathetic understanding between physics and spirituality, or more accurately between particle physics and mysticism: where Einstein meets God," Vanessa grinned.

"Now you've both lost me," sighed Gabby.

"I'm sorry," said Vanessa, "actually I had noticed your glazed expressions; we've reached a subject that is, for most people, very difficult to understand, but when you *feel* the subject, you discover you *know* all about it."

"What has Einstein got to do with spirituality and healing experiences?" asked Sophie.

"Einstein's gift to mankind is the knowledge and scientific fact that every aspect of the universe is a form of energy: everything in the world, including things that are substantial as well as elements that are ethereal, are all aspects of the same universal energy; some energy is solid matter - such as our body, but even parts of ourselves which are not solid – such as thoughts and emotions – are forms of energy which manifest at various levels depending upon their vibration."

"I understand that;" said Frank, seeming to awaken from his unhappy state, "in terms of physics, colour and sound are visible and audible vibrations of energy which, as you said, appear as an ascending order according to their frequency; and one of Einstein's theories explains how matter – such as our body – is actually energy compressed, it vibrates at a frequency lower than other aspects of our self. I think it's true that the vibration of sound disturbs the energy of matter, so I guess that's why you hummed - or toned - as Maria said, during my family's session with you."

"Indeed; some healers tone during a session, others work with the appearance of colour through the body, and some, in fact, see and hear nothing at all; there are also a few who do not need to be in close proximity to their client because their thought – even from a significant distance – effectively promotes healing.

All healers work towards an individual's well-being by bringing about change in the vibrational state of the energy in the body. I guess you can understand what I mean by 'changing state' when you think about how water can become ice or steam..."

"And in healin'," interrupted Maria, excitedly, "sumthin' like anger or fear can change to become sumthin' solidly bad for us in our body...

Oh, Frank," she wailed, suddenly losing her childlike happiness, "if only we could make Laura's cancer change from the painful stuff in her body into sumthin' that we could lift away, just like the sadness we moved out of Colin's dog."

Frank dropped his head into his hands, "Vanessa, in our session you gave me and my family those images, and today you've described how pictures help us to find spirit's wisdom; if... since... we are amazing... what causes me to feel so weak? Please help me to understand... is it that I must have complete trust in the process... or will absolute self-belief enable me to break free from my debilitating fear?"

"Sometimes trust and self-belief go a long way to help when you are in the midst of doubt and fear," said Vanessa, gently, "though the phenomenon of healing is actually quite independent of these characteristics; in one sense the concept of healing is somewhat easier to accept rather than trying to find trust or self-belief in the midst of turmoil, and yet in other ways healing is more problematic because there is no tangible explanation for its occurrence.

Let me try to explain further: in order to explore and use what is fundamentally true and naturally real you do not need to have trust, and neither is it essential to have confidence in the process; you see, when we utilise energy for healing we are actually using what comes naturally through us as a normal process of life.

For example, bamboo shoots do not need confidence or trust to become upright after being forced to the ground.

A seed does not need trust or belief in the 'nothing' which is at its centre; it naturally draws upon what is essentially itself in order to grow and blossom.

Once we cease trying to make faith, belief and morality a condition of our worldly success - or even of our healing – and when, instead, we discover our inherent value lies in the existence of our soul, then we begin to live as our natural spirit self, and as a result of our change in perception we relax knowing that we are simply a natural expression of life, like bamboo in the wind or waves of the sea, living in subtle synchronicity with the energy of the universe."

The sudden noise of the annex door slamming against its frame caused most of them to jump in surprise.

"He's gone again," muttered Colin. "I'm losing patience with Malcolm; he bolts each time he finds difficulty with the topic of our discussions."

"Laura's right about that situation," said Frank, continuing to regain his composure, "When I find the wherewithal to give more of my attention to our budding young people's group maybe it will help Malcolm's daughter through her adolescent crisis, then perhaps father and daughter will be reconciled.

Anyway, I'm beginning to feel less weak and somewhat more comforted by being with you all.

And, Vanessa, I assume I'm mistaken by continuing to feel anxious about my family's session with you? Tell me, is it possible for my own doubts to cause my wife's healing to fail?"

"During each session some form of healing always takes place on various levels of being," she replied.

"You can't guarantee a cure, then?" asked Colin, intently.

"It's never possible for a healer to predict the outcome of her work," said Vanessa. "In fact, there are instances of the most determined sceptics experiencing a cure, so I am certain that positive physical results do not depend on faith in an external power, belief in the process, nor in the perceived goodness of the recipient; but rest assured, Frank, the end results are not affected by the natural doubts of those hoping for a miracle."

"Then what will make it work? Laura's surely got the best possible help," said Gabby tearfully.

"It seems that success is not guaranteed by the integrity of healing or the urgency of loving friends; indeed, the whole phenomenon remains a mystery."

"I'm sure that's a great comfort for Frank...and Laura," muttered Colin, cynically.

"I do believe it has to do with readiness – just as you were emotionally and spiritually ready to meet me," said Vanessa directly. "It may also have something to do with the 'healee's' notion of life and living, and how a 'cure' may subsequently affect the healed person's psyche."

"What do you mean?" asked Frank, warily.

Vanessa moved to sit close to him, "There's no need to be afraid," she said, calmly, "Laura's personality is not at all like some individuals who would not have a clue what to do with the rest of their life if they experienced a cure: for some people, becoming the recipient of an amazing phenomenon causes them ever afterwards to believe that they must prove their worth through extraordinary living, and subsequently they feel forever indebted and unfulfilled.

Also, Laura is so different from some who are so shocked by a personal 'miracle' that they remain fearful for the rest of their life: for these people the occurrence of a perceived supernatural event causes an intolerable change in their perception of life, and so living becomes an inexplicable challenge.

In both these scenarios – with personalities which are fundamentally different from Laura's - any notion of a remarkable cure diminishes because the momentous event shatters any sense of what is possible, or indeed normal, so that the physical cure becomes an emotional or transpersonal nightmare, quite the opposite of what healing intends."

"Is it possible for science to prove that healing happens?" asked Frank, wearily.

"There are documented laboratory experiments which show how a healer's thought affects water which, when subsequently used to water plants, causes the nurtured specimens to grow somewhat larger and healthier than controlled examples, though I remain sceptical about the use of scientific measurement to prove healing phenomena..."

"I agree," said Colin, "particle physics was an unknown subject until scientists found a way to measure sub-atomic particles, so how is it possible to dismiss Vanessa's work simply because it cannot, at present, be measured?"

Gabby and Sophie exchanged glances: they were never quite sure which side of a controversy Colin might adopt, and they found it increasingly difficult to understand why he habitually expressed extremes of opinion normally opposed to his usual conservative views.

"I'm lost again," said, Maria. "It's time for a break; I've made some 'ealthy snacks, and we should all drink lots of water."

"Yes, please, I'm definitely in need of food now," said Frank, "I'm afraid I haven't eaten anything today; I just didn't feel like it earlier.

And when we resume, Vanessa, I'd really like you to talk more about what takes place during healing sessions so that I may understand more clearly what Laura and I can expect as a result of your work."

"And I'll go and find Malcolm," said Colin, sternly.

"I think it's best if *I* look for him," Vanessa replied, soothingly.

After a rather subdued break they all resumed their places ready to continue their challenging learning experience; surprisingly both Malcolm and Frank appeared more refreshed and decidedly less anxious.

"So, Vanessa," said Frank, "is healing *really* a matter of physics..."

"And not God," interrupted Colin, warily.

Vanessa winced and then closed her eyes, "A particle physicist and a mystic share a similar aim," she murmured cautiously, "they are each searching for the Ultimate. Both will experience wonder and awe throughout their explorations, and both understand the notion of oneness – the interconnectedness of all things – though the mystic appreciates his relationship with the Infinite and may yearn for union with the Divine.

A healer realises the same sense of unity, and naturally uses this truth to facilitate healing."

"What do you mean?" asked Maria.

"Remember the example of the light bulb?"

"If the wire connection is firm then the light is strong," said Sophie.

"Yes; and from the depth of his heart a healer knows, metaphorically speaking, that he shines very brightly as one of a series of lights connected to the source of power; he is also certain that everyone else is a brightly illumined bulb too; all are connected and have the power to shine, though many are unaware of their connection."

"So how does he use this awareness for healing?"

"His thought is the love which runs through the wires making the connective circuit; his love 'speaks' from his heart to the heart of his healee, and through the ethers of love he verifies the connection of them both with their source, reminding the client of something that he may have long forgotten - that he too is pure love."

"And does the healee's heart hear and answer?"

"It does: healer and healee are connected in the one eternal circuit, the healee's heart is of the same substance as the healer's; when the client realises this similarity he is 'sparked' back to his original bright light; you see, the healee is made aware that he is also connected to the same powerful source as the healer, so he is reminded of who he is and where he is at home."

"You mean, the healee learns that he is light and that he belongs in the string of bulbs together with everyone else?"

"Indeed: when the healee's heart hears and responds to the loving call, he understands who he is in relation to the source, and then he has opportunity to think about himself in relation to the ultimate power, and when he realises his light potential he reasserts his strong connection."

"That's when energy changes inside him?"

"Absolutely: where his energy had previously faltered, it changes and becomes stronger as a result of its firmer connection; then the body responds to the energetic change and begins self-repair; as a result, the vibrational frequency of the disease is shattered and a biological healing becomes possible."

"But during a session, do you as healer know you are enabling a cure?"

"Let's think again about Maria's description of the chakras: each chakra is a centre of energy and each vibrates at a different frequency; these are: the frequency of matter or the physical body, the frequency of emotions, the frequency of desires and the mind, and ultimately the frequency of the spirit. Indeed, the highest vibration – the one that is closest to The Ultimate – is that of Spirit.

Now, if a healer responds to her client using her emotions - feeling the desperate desire for her client to recover - she will be using the vibration of the emotional chakra, and her healing goals will function through the frequency of the physical body."

"So she will be thinking at the level of the client's base and second chakra," said Sophie.

"Which are of a *lower* frequency than the heart," added Frank.

"Indeed."

"And the lower chakras are farther away from spirit," said Maria, "farther away from the Ultimate."

"Ah ha."

"So the connection is weaker."

"And less likely to be effective."

"Exactly. So a proficient healer will avoid wishing for someone to be well, and does not dwell upon the physical ailments - even though she needs to have compassion for her client's suffering - but instead she naturally sends the power of unconditional love from her heart, sometimes through her hands, sometimes with a loving glance, and in a few cases simply through thought from a distance."

"It's a kind of prayer then," said Gabby.

"It is. Though it is 'pure' prayer, requesting whatever is for 'highest good' for the sick person; this is really prayer for their harmony with 'the All' rather than a request for a specific recovery; if prayer focusses upon a particular desire it becomes burdened with human emotion and disrupts the flow of pure love; so we could say it is better to be prayer-full – I mean, absolutely suffused with loving prayer - rather than to pray about a particular situation."

"I'm reminded of the expression on Maria's face that day with Colin's dog," murmured Frank, "it was a look of pure compassion."

"Sent authentically from an innocent soul who deep down knew her connection with the Divine, and therefore knew exactly what to do to heal the sick animal," said Vanessa, reverently.

"If only I knew what to do for poor Laura," Maria cried.

"We'll come to that in a moment," replied Vanessa, gently.

She continued, "This afternoon I brought you all a seed, hoping that you would receive it as a token of spiritual affirmation, and I wanted you to remember that it's normal for a seed, once it receives nurture, to use its own expression of life force to grow and develop, and eventually to recede and 'die'.

The seed does what comes naturally: I like to think that it is maintaining a state of 'being', and whenever difficulties occur in the natural world, life helps nature to recover itself; the same action occurs in healing: we are all capable of naturally recovering from disease to well-being.

Ultimately we react according to our perception of self and our relationship with the divine; a healthy response in both of these realms can be described as being 'whole'; and since healing brings an individual to a sense of well-being with himself, with others and with the creative source, I prefer to change the description of the process from 'healing' to 'wholeing', because at the 'end of the day', and at the end of life's day, the client - whether 'cured' or not - finds peace because they have been gifted the remembrance that they are whole: a magnificent shining bulb eternally connected to the ultimate power, forever at home.

And so, as we come to the end of a very long and intense session I'd like to emphasise once more how important it is for you to find simple ways of nurturing your natural self, to remind yourself that you are indescribable wondrous beings."

"I need to remember," murmured Frank.

"Remember your Self," affirmed Gabby.

"That makes an ideal mantra," said Sophie.

"A mantra? I can't remember what a mantra is," Maria frowned.

"It's a short phrase to repeat over and over again, a few words on which to concentrate so that you remain meditatively calm; it's a practice that helps to still your active mind, a personal phrase that makes you stop 'doing' so that you have a few minutes of just 'being' as Vanessa might say!" Gabby replied, enthusiastically.

"I'm definitely in need of a mantra, then!"

"Not just you, Maria; we all need moments of calm," murmured Colin, humbly.

"And I like the phrase Gabby has suggested," remarked Vanessa. "It's interesting that the words may be interpreted in at least three different ways:

Remember your SELF - remind yourself of who you really are and know yourself as spirit.

RE-member your self - be aware of all your aspects: body, mind, emotions and spirit and have them brought together, or re-membered, as one entity under the direction of your soul.

Remember YOURSELF - put yourself first, so that you are always well-prepared to help others."

"I don't like the third idea," said Gabby, impatiently. "We shouldn't put ourselves first because it is selfish behaviour; I've always assumed that it's good manners and respectful to put others first, though I admit it's never satisfied me."

"I don't think it's selfish, Gabby," said Sophie, gently. "I'm reminded of the safety instructions passengers are given on an aircraft: When in difficulty we're told to reach for our own oxygen mask before helping others; this really makes sense to me, not only when I'm travelling, but also in everyday life - it's important for me to attend to myself first so that I am better able to help my children."

"Have you noticed how your collective thoughts are naturally flowing from the deep well of wisdom?" Vanessa remarked. "It's wonderful that you're each discovering your perceptive self and allowing a natural flow of suggestions and advice; our group is certainly discovering oneness!

So now let's use Gabby's mantra in a meditative way: Close your eyes and notice how your abdomen rises and falls with your breath just like a gentle tide moving in and out; feel the motion of your breathing; listen to the sound of your breath moving in and out; keep watching and noticing, and when your mind wanders – and it definitely will wander! – gently bring your attention back to your breath…

Now, when you feel ready, begin to whisper the mantra:

Remember your SELF, RE-member your self, remember YOURSELF."

Gradually they joined in with low, murmuring voices:
"Remember your SELF"
"RE-member your Self"
"Remember YOURSELF"

Like the ticking of a clock and the swell of a gentle tide their breathing and murmuring continued until Vanessa quietly brought their meditation to a close:

"And now, all of you, please gradually return your mind to complete alertness, stretch your body and appreciate your natural way of being."

"Thank you, thank you, thank you all," said Frank, tearfully. "My situation may not have changed, but I feel much more assured and peaceful about the future – even though I'm still crying!"

"You have done well to share your vulnerability with us, Frank. And perhaps you will allow me to share Laura's situation with everyone?" said Vanessa.

Frank nodded.

She continued, "I know your thoughts have been with Laura over recent weeks, but now Frank and I would like you to intensify your loving attention as Laura goes for surgery and spends time in hospital. You know what to do: please set aside time each day to think about Laura; try not to imagine her situation or plan how you'd like her to recover, simply hold her in thought. You know the potential power of loving thought, and Laura will be aware of you reaching out to her.

Together we send loving thought to Laura... loving thought to Laura...loving thought to Laura..."

Their long and intense meeting ended somewhat sombrely as they hugged Frank and cried with him; and as they prepared to leave they confirmed their plans for the shared provision of meals and practical care for him and his children in the absence of the much loved wife and mother.

Chapter 12   Responsibility

Maria was content to assume the role of temporary surrogate Mum to Frank's children; she knew that Frank and his family were capable of cooking for themselves but it satisfied her to be of practical help by preparing meals in the Sputnik room. They quickly settled upon a routine of the two families eating together, and before long Colin took his place at the table where he tried to provide fatherly support for the weary Frank.

Their communal meals were a learning experience for Maria's children who discovered the novelty of eating together seated at the table and very quickly adopted the natural manners of Frank's family; in fact, for the first time in their lives they learned to show appreciation for their food, to help clear up after eating and to communicate without provoking each other.

Frank was grateful for the homely support, and confidently left his children in Maria's care, although his fatigue and anxiety made him less amenable to Colin's persistent enquiries.

Maria cautioned the old man, "You know, Colin, Frank appreciates your thoughtfulness, but he is just too full of worry to have you keep askin' him about Laura."

"I know, I know but I keep wondering what'll happen when she comes home," he said testily.

"When she comes home all will be well; we'll all get back to normal," Maria replied, briskly.

"Now, you know that won't happen," he muttered, "she'll return to him and those children in such an awful state, and they'll be left to manage by themselves."

"They'll never be by themselves with all of us ready to 'elp," said Maria, fiercely. "What has made you so miserable and unhelpful? We don't need this kind of talk, Colin, really we don't. And you mustn't speak like that in front of Frank; just stop botherin' him."

Colin persisted, "He'll be on his own at home, behind closed doors; he'll have to watch her go through so much agony; there'll be sickness, nurses taking over the house, all that nasty treatment; how do you think he'll face it all? Surely he's thought about these problems? What do you think he might do?"

"Do? DO? He'll love her, take care of her, and pray for her recovery, that's what he'll do...and we will too." She threw the tea cloth at him and continued to scold him as if she was speaking with her cantankerous, aging father, "Now stop being so mournful and 'elp me clear up; can't think what's the matter with you; it's time you asked Vanessa to 'elp you find your old self."

"My old self? I don't want to find my old self, and I don't want Vanessa, of all people, to see that side of me," he muttered, frantically.

Their conversation ended as the children rushed into the room.

Maria was glad that the two families, different though they were in temperament, ability and upbringing, had gelled into happy togetherness; she was thrilled to see the improvement in the behaviour of her brood, and comforted that Frank's children were distracted by the brusque personalities of their new friends: their interaction was definitely helping the anxious children through their difficult moments.

Her hectic days at Sputnik's Hub, together with her companionship with Colin, had temporarily taken her away from the enjoyable get-togethers that she had appreciated with Gabby and Sophie; however, Maria's growing self-confidence helped her to know that their maturing friendship was not dependent upon regular meetings, although periodically she was relieved to have their assistance in Sputnik's kitchen.

Sophie and Gabby regularly met in their respective homes and grew in appreciation of each other as they developed a joint venture within the Sputnik organisation. The centre continued to be a welcoming place for friendship and self-discovery despite its members' burden of compassionate concern for Laura and her family.

However, the popularity of Sputnik's Hub meant that occasionally - as small "fringe" groups - they sought alternative venues for sessions of intimate learning, and it was for one of these meetings that Gabby and Sophie were invited to Vanessa's home.

"Why do you think it feels so special at Vanessa's?" Sophie pondered as they strolled along the river path for the arranged meeting. "Do you think the peacefulness is simply because her home is isolated from the village in the depth of the countryside?"

"Possibly... Though countryside mud on the soles of my shoes is not the reason why I remove them at her front door! Her home feels sacred, a sort of comfortable retreat, a place for soul searching," Gabby replied.

"Yes, I think you're right: Vanessa's home is her sanctuary, so it's natural that it becomes a peaceful refuge for us too."

"Umm, and I suspect the tranquil atmosphere inside the cottage is created because of the way she treats her surroundings," Gabby mused. "Her home is as neat and tidy as mine, but it takes frenetic work for me to make things nice, whereas she acts with love towards everything around her: she has a sort of *reverence* for her home which makes the rooms feel calm and satisfying."

"I agree. The love she has for her home is not materialistic; it's because of her close rapport with worldly things: she *feels* the connection – it's all about 'oneness', she said to me the other day – which means she doesn't see herself separate or detached from anything, even her furniture and furnishings!"

"What else did she say?"

"That everything has 'consciousness' because everything comes from 'one source': she is convinced that most things – even though they appear inanimate - have some sense of awareness. I've heard about people who talk to plants, but Vanessa likes to interact with almost everything – even food and clothes!"

"Trouble is, there are times when her ideas make complete sense to me, and her behaviour is contagious! For instance, this morning I found myself contemplating what colour underwear I should choose for today, and then I asked my body what it would like for dinner this evening!"

Sophie laughed, "Yes, you are beginning to sound like Vanessa! But however odd her ideas seem, they do make you feel better about yourself in the world – sort of less alone and separate, and more 'at home' – don't they?"

"Absolutely," Gabby agreed, as they reached Vanessa's door.

"Come in, come in, it is good to see you," Vanessa's girlish excitement was very different from her usual measured tone of greeting, "I have a surprise for you later; you will be so pleased!"

Gabby and Sophie exchanged glances; they sensed a side of Vanessa's personality they hadn't previously experienced and wondered what could have brought such delight.

"It's good of you to let us meet here," Gabby began with her usual nervous chatter.

"Now relax, both of you; I want you to feel at home. We won't be disturbed...not for a while, anyway!" she grinned. "Let's have some tea and talk through some of the issues that continue to trouble you both; you know, even though you have different challenges, I think their resolution will come from addressing the same fundamental struggle."

Vanessa's direct approach continued to surprise the women even though they had become used to her penetrating, no-nonsense manner of speaking; nonetheless, like most visitors to the home, Sophie and Gabby instantly felt at ease and ready to unravel the mystery of their inter-personal difficulties.

"Well, my struggle continues to be with myself," laughed Gabby self-consciously. "I know it's me: I drive myself to desperation because of my obsessive way of managing my home; and 'struggle' is definitely the word for my continuing attempts to communicate with my daughter; I've recently learned that I've driven my husband away completely, and it's likely I will do the same with my granddaughter when she is old enough to choose."

Vanessa's expression showed the compassion she felt for the confused, sad and lonely woman; she reached out to hold Gabby's trembling hand and immediately calmed the torrent of self-criticism: "Your account makes it easy for us to work together," she murmured, "many people are reluctant to speak of their difficulties, and those who do, usually claim that the issues are about everyone else! So you are well on the way to self-understanding and healing."

Momentarily embarrassed by her friend's outpouring, Sophie also began to disclose feelings of inadequacy: "For a while I haven't felt as comfortable with my husband as I used to, though I don't see how Gabby and I need the same kind of help, even though, like her, I believe my difficulties with relationships are my fault.

Actually, you both know that my biggest problem continues to be how I feel about Julie, who used to be my best friend: she and I haven't spoken for weeks and it's embarrassing how we ignore each other at the school gate; some days I feel sick with apprehension, and I have no idea what I did wrong."

Vanessa leaned back in her chair, paused to sip her tea, took a deep breath and closed her eyes. Gabby and Sophie glanced at each other; they recognised Vanessa's preparatory ritual before teaching, and they too settled into their chairs and closed their eyes; the atmosphere in the room was of tranquil contentment, yet eager anticipation.

"First let us set aside any notion of self-blame," she said, firmly. "Whilst it is wise to look within for self-correction, it is a mistake to blame yourself and to frame the problem in terms of it being your fault. Your difficulties are not your fault and you are not to blame, but you do have the wisdom to understand your inter-personal challenges, and the power to change your way of being."

"We've talked to each other about our problems," said Gabby, "and we've both been trying to change, but we think it might help if you tell us whether there's a particular reason for the way we behave."

"That's why we're glad you invited us to your home," added Sophie, with sudden nervousness.

"It delights me to have you come with an enquiring mind and open heart to work with me here," Vanessa responded, fondly.

"Although you must be very busy with people coming to seek your help," Sophie chatted, trying to mask her rising anxiety.

Vanessa opened her eyes and gazed at the floor, "To speak of being busy is such a sad remark," she murmured. "People hide behind the assertion of being busy for a variety of reasons: sometimes to give an impression of self-importance, occasionally to avoid gifting time to be with others and frequently to avoid simply 'being' because they dread the consequences of having nothing to do."

Her clouded expression gave Sophie more concern, "Oh," she gulped, "I'm so sorry to have upset you."

"And that's another expression which needs some clarification," said Vanessa, gently. "Dear Sophie, *you* have not upset me: it's important to learn that other people's feelings are not created by whatever you choose to say; on the contrary, everyone else must take personal responsibility for the way they react to you and your words."

The two women frowned in consternation, "I'm beginning to feel quite troubled," said Sophie, "and I'm not sure why. I've been looking forward to coming to see you, but now I feel anxious and actually a little afraid."

"And both of us are trembling," added Gabby, "although I am sure I'm perfectly safe here."

"Let me assure you both: there is no need to feel anxious about this healing session; though if you feel you would rather not continue we may simply enjoy our tea and chat together while we await..."

"No, no," Sophie interrupted, "I definitely want to continue because I need to understand the cause of my anxiety."

"And I will be glad not only to help you understand, but also to relieve you of your anxious fear," said Vanessa, gently. "Let me unravel the reason for your rising concern: during our conversation you mistakenly believed that you had caused me to be upset, and as a well-meaning, loving person you are naturally distressed at the idea of making someone unhappy."

"Especially you, Vanessa," she interrupted, "and particularly in your own home!"

Vanessa bowed her head in acknowledgement, and continued, "And you were confused by my comment that your words do not cause another's upset."

"Yes," Gabby responded, "your explanation doesn't make sense because you were clearly bothered when Sophie suggested you might be busy."

"And since I brought up the topic..." Sophie persisted.

"You felt *responsible* for my disquiet."

"Yes. It was my fault."

"Ahh!" exclaimed Vanessa, "Is that so?"

"*That's* our problem, isn't it? It's simple: we blame ourselves for other people's reactions, when really we should just shrug our shoulders and let them think what they like!" Gabby exclaimed.

Vanessa paused and cautiously replied, "Well, gradually, as you notice the dynamics of your interactions, and after we have completed some energy work, you will no longer have the 'problem' as you call it.

But I should also point out that there's an additional reason for the rising anxiety in you both: your inner self is more than a little anxious about today's anticipated healing work."

"Oh! That's another of my ongoing problems," said Gabby. "I suppose my ego self is concerned about what's going to happen during this session; I clearly remember that was the reason why I nearly missed one of our planned meetings at Sputnik's Hub!"

"Is my ego worried too?" asked Sophie, "Because I'm not aware of it; I just feel upset about having made you sad."

"You're rarely upset for the reason you think," Vanessa replied. "And, to confirm, I believe the actual reasons for your current disquiet are these: your inner selves know that you are to receive remarkable healing today, so naturally you feel 'on edge'; the healing will be about adjusting your perception of self which at present is dominated by low self-esteem, and this makes you feel uneasy in strange places; low self-esteem causes you to be concerned about what others think of you, and subsequently makes you want to please me; and this results in increased anxiety when you mistakenly believe you have caused me to be upset."

"That's a whole tummy-full of upset," said Sophie, "no wonder I began to feel afraid!"

"Indeed. And amongst all these challenges it is important that you understand the difference between the notion that you *made* me upset, and the fact that you *said* something to which I have a choice of how I may react.

You mistakenly assume that the reaction of others is a direct result of your comments; you make other people's behaviour your responsibility, which means that you take on an inappropriate burden; this causes additional emotional strain so that ultimately you blame yourself for any subsequent difficulties in the relationship."

"My head is spinning, Vanessa," Sophie exclaimed. "Please explain again how such a simple conversation between us has sent my feelings spiralling out of control."

"I'm sorry that you feel confused," said Vanessa, gently. "Gabby suggested that the problem is simple; in fact, the issue is deeply seated in our psyche and causes much unhappiness between many people, so it is worth closely re-examining our innocent conversation so that we may tease out the reason for its emotional charge."

She took time to focus upon her breathing and then again closed her eyes, "Sophie, your comment about being busy was followed by my gloomy reaction; when you saw my expression you felt responsible so you became anxious and uncomfortable; the situation became an unnecessary whirlpool of emotions which could have resulted in a further round of recrimination.

The interplay of behaviour causes you to blame yourself and exacerbates your inherent low self-esteem; and so now our healing aim must be for you to learn how to work from inner calm assurance knowing that you may say anything to anyone from your heart and allow them to respond according to their choice: they have an *ability* to *respond*, which means you do not need to assume *responsibility* for them."

"I don't know how Sophie is feeling," said Gabby, anxiously, "but I'm really not sure about this: once more I'm struggling to accept what you say."

"Well," Vanessa responded, "let's examine the alternatives; our unhealthy scenario is this: Sophie's comment about being busy reminded me of my sadness that many people have little interest in listening to their spirit self; she saw my expression, felt guilty about 'making' me upset and became overly concerned, blaming herself for my unhappiness.

Whereas a healthy scenario of the same event is this: Sophie should confidently and freely speak from her heart, knowing that I am free to express my emotions and capable of dealing with any personal sadness.

Our interaction may still bring up expressions of sadness, but the situation is not made worse by feeling responsible, nor complicated by self-blame, guilt and remorse. Instead both of you might healthily acknowledge my unhappy response and open your heart to me with unconditional love."

"What causes us to immediately lurch into the unhealthy way of taking responsibility instead of allowing others their 'ability to respond'?" asked Sophie.

"You may be relieved to know that the fundamental cause is to be found in almost everyone."

"You mean, most people behave and feel like I do?" asked Gabby with amazement.

"To a greater or lesser degree, indeed they do; however, some find ways of hiding the problem and are skilled at avoiding personal issues, and many develop strategies to cope so that the rest of the world never discovers their secret."

"What secret?"

"The secret to which we keep returning: lack of self-confidence, feeling unworthy, constantly in need of reinforcement and frequently seeking the approval of others. The mistake is held by most of us, although with determination we keep our low self-esteem hidden.

We nurture the mistaken idea that we are lacking something of infinite importance, we are not sure what it is, and we live with the subliminal fear of being helpless; we exist with a secret need for the assistance of someone more powerful whom we hope will eventually make us feel complete."

"Are you talking about God?" Gabby frowned, "Because honestly He deserted me long ago."

"Well, our relationship with God, a Higher Power, or whatever term we choose to use, certainly affects the way we feel about ourselves," said Vanessa, "and it is a topic we should discuss at some point; but for the moment let's continue to explore what happens when individuals persist in their search for external help."

"I'm sure we both need an explanatory story," Sophie grinned, as her anxiety began to subside.

"All right! Let's consider the behaviour of children as they gradually discover friendship: usually they begin school with friends they have known almost from birth; their friendship groups develop and often remain strong throughout school; sometimes they are constant for life.

However, on occasions, when a new child moves into the area, friendship groups undergo change, particularly when individuals are fascinated by a new arrival: existing relationships may break up because some children behave with exaggerated kindness towards the new friend.

This dynamic happens because some personalities become overly interested and excited by what they see as a novel situation: they anticipate that a different person will add something special to their lives.

The exaggerated interest in the stranger continues until the children realise that there is really nothing unusual about the newcomer; eventually the child is integrated into the class and the novelty is forgotten; nevertheless, the subliminal search for someone new continues because of people's desire to find something external - something other than what they believe themselves to be - to make themselves feel complete."

Sophie's vacant expression suggested that she was lost in thought, "That is exactly how Julie reacted when our new neighbour arrived," she murmured. "She behaved in such an extraordinarily friendly way towards the other parent at the school gate and totally ignored me! But we are not children! Why couldn't we all have been friends together? I shared so much with Julie: told her my secret fears and poured out my worries; and now I feel really betrayed."

"Well, I think that your relationship with Julie has been affected by her insecurities," said Vanessa, opening her eyes. "And these are what we have been discussing: lack of self-worth – in Julie's case the impact of this was lessened by keeping you as a dependent friend; and the mistaken belief that she is separate and alone: so she clings to the idea that she is an essential part of other people's existence, and she tries to ensure that her life revolves around people who make her feel complete and fulfilled."

"So Julie feels inadequate and is searching for something or someone other than me to make her feel special?"

"It's highly likely," replied Vanessa, "particularly when you are certain that no disagreement forced you apart."

"How may the difficulty be resolved?"

"Well, ultimately, we'll all be healed of this perceived inadequacy when we eventually come to the realisation that we are beautiful expressions of thought and emotion wrapped around a miraculous body and enveloped by our spirit or soul, and when we also accept that we have everything we need within us, because - as our spirit self - we are an absolute expression of everything; then we will understand that we are whole, without the need for anyone or anything to make us complete."

"And I suppose God has a role in fulfilling our 'complete' self," said Gabby, suspiciously.

"For the moment I'm still trying to avoid any discussion about God, because when we begin to share ideas about The Divine's place in our life our thoughts and emotions can become very confused - our wires become crossed, so to speak - unless we've had the opportunity to debate the concept and have an appreciation of what we mean when we speak of 'God'.

Such a discussion will be thought-provoking and enjoyable, especially with a heart open in trust and mutual understanding; but, for today, let's firmly establish the foundations of interpersonal understanding before we take on the transpersonal!"

"I think Gabby's feeling irritated," remarked Sophie, as she glanced towards her friend, "and I haven't a clue what you mean by transpersonal."

"It means us and God," said Gabby sullenly. "I've always had concerns that the Sputnik group would eventually become religious."

"But that's not at all what Vanessa is saying, Gabby: she's trying to stop you talking about God so that we can get on with finding out about people first."

Vanessa's laughter filled the room making it impossible for Gabby and Sophie not to join in.

"So, may we continue to discuss people?" she asked.

"It might be good to have another of your stories," Gabby said, somewhat more cheerfully.

"Yes, I'm sure! So I'd like you to imagine that the centre of your being is like a ring dough-nut, spongy and expanding at its edge, but with an empty centre - a hole - at its middle."

The women giggled at Vanessa's unusual imagery.

"Bear with me," she smiled, "remember I'm used to teaching young children!"

"Well, we are children at heart!"

"Indeed. I'm glad you are! However, let's pursue the image: We humans have a desperate urge to fill the dough-nut hole, and sometimes we think we can achieve this by trying very hard to do good things."

"Like me," said Gabby.

"Then there are people who seek out someone in desperate need of help, and discover that their dough-nut expands with the thrill of giving support. The needy person creates a wonderful distraction from their own problems; the dough increases and the hole diminishes; so in a perverse way it is beneficial to have a friend's dependency."

"Oh, just like Julie and me: I was in such despair when I lost my babies, and terrified through my successful pregnancies in case they ended in grief too; Julie encouraged me to talk and cry, and do more talking and crying... I thought she loved me."

"She probably does love you," assured Vanessa. "But recently you have grown stronger with less need to share and cry."

"So Julie's dough-nut hole was not being filled!"

"Exactly. Until a new neighbour arrived, and, like the children I described earlier, Julie's subconscious mind sought out the newcomer who, she supposed, might give her answers or at least satisfy her need to have someone fill an inner void."

"What must I do about Julie?"

"Do you feel ready to address the issue right now?"

"I'll go outside for a walk while you two work together," Gabby suggested.

"No, please stay," Sophie urged her friend, "I can't think there'll be anything private or personal, in fact I still can't think why the problem has occurred at all."

Vanessa moved to sit beside Sophie; they both settled back on the sofa and closed their eyes.

"Dear Sophie, first, let's focus upon breathing; notice the movement of your tummy as you breathe in...and out... Listen to the sound of your breath in... and out...

And now focus your attention upon your heart ..."

"It's bright in front of my closed eyes, as if the sun is shining, but I know there's no sunlight in this room at the moment."

"Indeed. Your heart is wide open, beaming out your love to all who come close. Are you ready for Julie to come close to you?"

"I think so...yes...I've just noticed I no longer feel anxious; in fact I'm extremely calm and settled...thank you."

"You're most welcome! Now we invite the spiritual consciousness of Julie to come and greet Sophie; we ask this for the highest good of both Julie and Sophie and with the complete assurance that both young ladies are safe and free from censure..."

"We're sitting together on grass in the sunshine!" interrupted Sophie, excitedly, "I can see her quite clearly; we're like little girls making daisy chains!"

"A happy scene!" remarked Vanessa. "Now, Sophie, imagine that you are seated on the grass inside an imaginary circle, and that Julie is surrounded by her own circle. Both of you are seated totally within your own boundary, but the circles meet as they make a figure 8."

"Our boundaries are made of daisies!" Sophie smiled.

"Good! Now, speak with Julie in thought: while your heart is open and you're safely enclosed within your daisy boundary explain how you feel about the situation at the school gate, be honest and have the courage to 'speak your mind'; it's not necessary to speak out loud; take your time and ask her to listen without interruption or judgement..."

Vanessa opened her eyes to monitor her healee's progress, and after a few minutes Sophie nodded that she had finished her dialogue.

"Now, Sophie, ask Julie to tell you whatever she needs to in response to your words. Wait and give her time to talk..."

"She's hanging her head and fiddling with the daisies."

"Give her time..."

"She says she has nothing to tell me, she looks like a very small, lonely child, and now she tells me that her chest hurts – actually she's pointing to her heart."

"What would you like to do about that?"

"I'd like to help her feel better; it's strange but at this moment I feel as though I am her mother; I'd like to do the same for her as I do for my own little girl when she's unhappy...I'd like to hug her..."

"All right. With the understanding that your conscious selves remain healthily discrete, you may invite her spirit self to cross the circle boundary...allow her to come to you and draw her into your arms as if she is your daughter..."

"She's growing smaller in my arms!"

"Then maybe she's small enough to enter your heart?"

"Yes."

"Then with compassion and unconditional love, in the safety of pure healing, you may draw her into your heart...

How do you feel?"

"Complete and content...but strangely the scene in my mind has returned to our figure 8 daisies on the grass...we're back in our original positions, and now she wants me to reach across into her circle..."

"Do you feel confident to do that?"

"Yes. Sometimes my daughter draws me under her covers at bedtime to give me a sleepy hug...it feels the same...and now I feel that I am becoming small enough to step into Julie's heart...it's bright and comfortable...it feels just like my heart."

"Beautiful. Wisdom has shown you that we are all the same at our love-filled core.

And having completed this profound mutual opening of the heart, you will see that whatever is realised in spirit will come to be known and appreciated when you meet face to face."

"So does that mean it will be easier for me to meet Julie at the school gate tomorrow?"

"Well, I'm sure it will be easier for *you* to be your natural self with her, and it is up to Julie to choose what her face-to-face response will be...and I will eagerly await our next meeting to learn how the situation is resolved."

"And I'll try not to appear too interested when I'm at the school gate awaiting my granddaughter!" exclaimed Gabby.

Vanessa allowed her hand to linger over Sophie's heart; for a while they remained in quiet reflection until

Vanessa brought the healing experience to a close: "We thank the consciousness of Julie for being spiritually present and for her open-hearted response to her friend's invitation.

And I now command that spirit consciousness is perfectly, healthily and totally returned to their respective whole selves.

And so it is."

Sophie and Vanessa stretched and took deep breaths, and Gabby quietly sighed as if she had slept through Sophie's healing experience.

"We must have a break," said Vanessa, brightly. "I have some new plants to show you outside…"

They strolled in Vanessa's small garden, breathed the warm air and lifted their faces toward the sun until they felt ready to return to the sitting room and resume their work.

"What about me?" asked Gabby, impatiently, "I've been thinking about the image of the hole in the middle of the dough-nut. Do I have one?"

"I think you know the answer to that!" Vanessa smiled, "And you also know why."

"I think I have a very large hole and it's there because of what I described earlier: I've grown up believing I'm not good enough, and – to use your example - my father constantly reminded me of the hole in my centre; I've been trying to fill it by attempting to make things right, hoping to create a neat house, expecting to be a good mother...and grandmother..."

"And all the effort actually made your centre larger and more stretched so that you became weary with trying; weariness may have made you irritable and less easy to live with, and perhaps this contributed to your husband's decision to leave you."

"What about my husband?" Sophie interrupted, "Do you think he might be experiencing similar frustrations with me?"

"The image of the dough-nut hole may be applied to many couples who try very hard to please each other, and when they realise that their partner does not fill the inner void, they grow apart; sometimes one, or both, wander to 'pastures new' thinking that someone else may fill the empty space.

However, Sophie, there is something more significant that I must help you heal, though this may need to be addressed when you and I are alone."

"No, not at all," Sophie assured her. "If you both don't mind I'd like to continue now, and I'm very happy for Gabby to stay with me: I've grown close to her and I trust you both. In fact, you've said that we learn from each other, and when one person is helped it is as if all are healed."

"Indeed. You've adopted a wise attitude to healing, so let's proceed with what will be a *combined* session of spiritual energy work."

They settled deeper into their chairs, but as Vanessa prepared to begin they heard a tap at the door and two voices called:

"Hello?"

"We're here!"

"At last!" Vanessa exclaimed, "You'll both be so thrilled to see who's at the door!"

Chapter 13 Womenkind

"Vanessa?"

"Are you there?"

"Are we too early?"

Gabby and Sophie opened their eyes wide with astonishment.

"That sounds like Frank..." said Sophie.

"With Laura," gasped Gabby.

"We're in here, come right in, your timing is perfect," Vanessa shouted. "I knew you two would be surprised," she added excitedly.

They gently hugged Laura and tearfully embraced Frank, who rapidly explained the situation: "Vanessa invited Laura to stay here to recuperate after her surgery; we both accepted with immense gratitude. Vanessa's hospitality means that for the time being Laura can receive home-care nursing here; she will be able to recover peacefully away from the children, and they and I may easily visit for durations of time that Laura can cope with."

"And I get to be near you all, under Vanessa's healing care, until I am ready to fully resume life with my family," added Laura. "And when Vanessa told us that you two were due here, I wanted to join you for what I hope will be a healing time just for women," she glanced at Frank.

"Yes, yes I'm going," he responded dutifully, "though I can hardly bear to be away from you... I'm so, so happy...

I'll just take your things up to your temporary bedroom..."
he looked to Vanessa for her approval, "...then I'm going to
meet the kids from school and have a bumper feast with
Maria and some of the gang at Sputnik's Hub." Again he
hugged Gabby and Sophie, and gently kissed his wife.

Before leaving he followed Vanessa as she moved
away from the animated group; he joined her in prayerful
thought and held her for some time in an appreciative heart-
to-heart embrace.

After Frank had gone the ladies tried to recover their
composure although Laura's earlier than expected discharge
from hospital had shocked the already anxious friends;
gradually their emotions changed to a sense of contented joy
as they recognised that the previously haggard figure of their
friend had returned to them substantially transformed: Laura
was now noticeably relieved and calm.
    "It's *so* good to see you and to have you back where
you belong...with your family and amongst us," said Gabby.
    "And looking so well, too," added Sophie,
appreciatively.

Vanessa's planned healing work with Sophie was put
on hold so that they could listen to Laura's extensive
description of her experience in hospital, her treatment, her
physical reactions, her fears and her more recent challenges
after having had surgery.

Sophie and Gabby were surprised how much energy Laura seemed to have as she talked in detail about the processes she had been through, but Vanessa was aware that Laura's outpouring was a significant part of her healing process.

However, they were all unprepared not only for Laura's continued candour as she described her experiences but also for her abrupt behaviour as her frenetic chatter subsided:

"I'm going through what most women in my situation face," she smiled bravely through trembling lips. "It took a while before I could look... and it hurt to see Frank's shocked reaction... then I couldn't bear to listen to his haltingly brave efforts to tell me it doesn't really matter. I've been angry...and sad...pathetic...and occasionally strong. I ought to be grateful for life... I am grateful, really, but my daily shower torments me.

You're all healthy ladies, and you are my true friends, so I want your honest opinion: after what surgeons have removed, am I still a woman, do you think?"

She dramatically lifted her sweater to reveal her scarred chest, "Look what I now lack after surgeons finished with me," she whispered, "and I have nothing left 'lower down' either."

Gabby and Sophie suppressed their shock, and breathed deeply to remain focussed upon Laura and her "empty" chest, for she was intent on them commenting upon the site of her mastectomy.

175

She repeated her question, "I want to know if I'm still a woman. What do you think?"

"First of all, Laura, I'm glad you've been brave enough to show me," said Gabby in a forced matter-of-fact tone.

"Me too," added Sophie. "If you don't mind me saying, I expected a flat chest after such an operation, not hollow and sort of caved in. I agree, you are brave showing us, and I feel honoured to have learned so much in a few seconds."

"Learned so much? What do you mean?" Laura queried.

Sophie began to cry, "I can hardly describe what happened just at the moment you lifted your sweater - it occurred so quickly, I was unprepared - but at that moment, or within a split second of your action, I saw an intense light shining above your head; it beamed through your body and came out through your heart, then almost blindingly it shone straight at me. Honestly, that's what I saw... it's true... and I can't help crying... I'm sure it was your spirit shining out at me; Laura, you've shown me... LOVE. I'm crying... but I feel overwhelming joy."

Their gathering had been focussed upon Laura in the midst of her personal and physical struggle, but immediately Vanessa's attention was drawn to Sophie's need, and once again she moved to sit beside her; taking hold of her trembling hand she affirmed the experience for them all:

"Let's give thanks for Laura's presence – safely returned to us, and for Sophie's experience of her Presence – her revealed spirit. And as we close our eyes we welcome the bright light as it continues to shine around us: Light from above descends through our crown and we feel the same joy as it is greeted by the Light that permanently nestles in our heart.

Let's breathe deeply and allow the light to continue to permeate our body, our emotions and our mind; and being suffused with light, we breathe it with ease because it is part of us - our inner-most being, and we send it out to those who are ready to receive."

Vanessa slowly moved from the sofa to stand behind Sophie; she opened her arms as if to embrace her, "Sophie, as you continue to breathe light, I believe this is an appropriate moment to send light to your dear deceased babies. They are here, in front of you; be happy to draw them to your breast; imagine you are feeding them, as indeed you would have done had they lived…"

Sophie nodded, and Gabby watched as her friend appeared to be suckling imaginary babies; she was intensely moved at the expression of maternal love on Sophie's face; Gabby glanced up at Vanessa, who nodded her acknowledgement, "Now, Sophie, feel free to draw your two nurtured babies towards your heart; enfold them and bring them deep into your centre; and now, for a few moments, please continue to breathe light into yourself and exhale it to the world."

Vanessa's hands hovered over Sophie, and then slowly she moved to give healing attention to Gabby.

Standing behind her, she said, "Dear Gabby, it's time to cease your debilitating effort, time to stop trying; breathe light into yourself and send it out, imagine you are in the presence of the family you have been trying so hard to please; notice them as they stand near you: your father is immediately in front of you, your husband is behind him, your daughter to one side, and your granddaughter behind her."

Gabby nodded and breathed deeply; her expression suggested that she felt calm and empowered, no longer fearing her father's criticism.

"Now," continued Vanessa, "as you breathe light in and out, focus your attention upon your family and watch as they gradually become smaller and smaller in front of you - so small that they each become the size of a foetus; as you notice them, and if you feel able, bring each of them to your breast and draw them into your heart."

"My father is first," said Gabby in a clear voice, "Dad, I forgive you. Now my husband: he may come into my heart because I forgive him too. But my daughter and granddaughter are not moving..."

"Well," said Vanessa, "you might think of someone else who needs your forgiveness first."

"Who? You mean me? Do I need to forgive myself?"

"Try and see."

"How? I don't know how."

"Simply announce it," murmured Vanessa.

"Alright. I am Gabrielle. I am beautiful light and I forgive myself...

Now I feel complete with all my family nestled in my heart."

The others spontaneously copied her affirmation:

"I am Sophie. I am beautiful light and I forgive myself."

"I am Laura. I am beautiful light and I forgive myself."

"I am Vanessa. I am beautiful light and I forgive myself."

Vanessa moved to stand behind Laura; she moved her hand to allow her palm to hover over the places where Laura had received surgery; and for some time she gave attention to the rest of Laura's body, sometimes toning, sometimes commenting on the colour of energy she perceived, and for a while she was quiet as her hands continued her dedicated work.....

Then she spoke authoritatively, "And now, Laura, take a moment to consider as you perceive your 'real' self; ask yourself the same searching question: Am I still a woman?"

Laura's face glowed serenely, "Yes; oh yes!" she breathed, "I'm still a woman; in fact I'm more than I previously thought: I may have physical pieces missing, but at this moment I feel absolutely complete."

Vanessa smiled, "May I place an imaginary mirror before you?"

"Yes, please."

"I invite you to see yourself in your mind's eye – as God sees you. Tell us Laura, what do you see?"

"Actually, the mirror shows me exactly as I am – scarred and caved in at my breast and tummy; but strangely, I don't mind what I see; in fact I find myself staring and examining my surgery wounds.

I imagine my surgeon appearing in the mirror; he's arrived to survey his work... he looks pleased... and I am too. For the first time I feel able to thank him and feel truly grateful for what he's removed – the disease and my feminine organs. Thank you, sir, thank you."

"Is there a reflection of anyone else in your mirror?"

"Yes, now the surgeon has gone, Frank's there, standing behind me."

"What does he say?"

"Nothing."

"Nothing?"

"That's right: when Frank and I are intimately together he is a man of very few words. And at this moment, in the mirror of my imagination, he reaches for my shoulders and turns me round to face him, and then he kisses each part of my wounded body."

"Laura, that's beautiful," Sophie whispered.

"Perhaps one day he'll be able to do that with you 'face to face' - do you think?" asked Gabby, respectfully.

"He already has," murmured Laura.

They sat in silent contemplation, appreciating the intimate stillness of love.

Vanessa brought them water, and after a while Gabby and Sophie prepared to leave; no words seemed appropriate, so after long and meaningful hugs they left Laura in the care of her healer.

"You know what?" said Gabby after they had been walking for a while.

"What?" Sophie responded.

"The light you saw around Laura; I think it was from God."

"Umm. I do too. God inside, God around and God above; and do you know how it makes me feel?"

"How?"

"Like a filled dough-nut."

"Whole."

"That's right! Whole...just like Laura."

Chapter 14   Active Wholeness

Sophie wasn't sure whether her restless night was due to her usual state of continued anxiety, her apprehension about further silent school gate encounters with Julie or her excited anticipation of a positive outcome of her work with Vanessa.

However, she was disappointed and surprised that Julie was not at the school gate as usual and was nowhere to be seen on the route to or from school that morning.

"Perhaps the children are sick," she said, as she and Gabby met for their usual working coffee meeting.

Their days were now becoming filled by appointments with women in the community who sought Gabby's advice on creating healthy homes where rooms could be subtly changed through the use of colour and tasteful fabrics to make either stimulating or relaxing environments, and with young mothers who appreciated Sophie's method of showing them how to be calm and thoughtfully connected to their babies and toddlers.

"Umm, there is a virus that's running its course through school," Gabby replied, "though it's doubtful that all of Julie's family would be affected at the same time. Perhaps her ego self couldn't face your wholeness!" she added mischievously.

"Aren't we being just a tiny bit catty?" Sophie grinned. "Let's forget about her and get on with our planning."

When Sophie met her son at the end of the school day she discovered that all of Julie's children had been absent, but as they made their way home she was shocked to find her former friend waiting outside her house.

Sophie's son was delighted to see his play-mate and they noisily kicked their football across the garden while Julie's girls happily played with Sophie's daughter. The visiting children showed no sign of any illness which would have accounted for their absence from school, but Sophie quickly decided that it was best to avoid the subject.

"How are you, Julie? It's been a long time since our children have played together at home, though I know the boys are still firm friends at school," she said, meaningfully.

Inwardly she reminded herself to relax by taking measured deep breaths just as she had practiced during meditation, and was surprised to realise how calm and strong the exercise made her feel as she continued to question her visitor:

"Is there something wrong? Something that I may help you with?"

"Wrong? Oh umm, no; nothing's wrong, well err...not really. It's just that I thought you might have my kids for a sleep over..."

"Of course, what date did you have in mind?"

"Well, today...this evening... I was thinking I could leave them here now."

"*Now!* Umm...I am rather busy... Well, no, not busy... What I actually meant to say was that I'm sure we can come to some arrangement... Is there some kind of emergency?"

"Emergency? Well...yes...it's my Mother...she's not well...so I need to go and see her."

"I'm so sorry," murmured Sophie. "Would you like to come inside for a minute; you do seem rather on edge; perhaps time for a cup of tea? Or is the emergency critical?"

"That's just like you!" Julie's emotions suddenly erupted, "always mumbling and asking questions. I thought you'd be helpful. You've become haughty and distant, and you haven't bothered to speak to me ever since you became part of that Sputnik thingy," her face grew red as she angrily drew her children away from their play.

"That's not how it was at all!" said Sophie, indignantly. "Please, wait... I'm sure it'll be fine to leave the children here..."

"Don't bother, I can manage by myself," Julie yelled as she marched away with her family.

Sophie sat at the kitchen table with her head in her hands and began to tremble, "That's not how it was meant to be," she muttered out loud.

"What, Mummy? Why can't they stay and play?" her disappointed son sighed.

"Perhaps they will, when their Grandma is feeling better."

And then, continuing to talk to herself she repeated, "You're never angry for the reasons you think... you're never angry for the reasons you think."

"Yes Mummy, but I'm hungry; is it time to eat now?"

Throughout the early evening Sophie had time to ponder the exchange with Julie while she attended to her children and finally settled them into bed. Her husband's long hours meant that she rarely expected him home until near their own bedtime.

However, she was surprised when he walked in the door somewhat earlier than usual, "Hello Sweetie, had a good day?" he asked, stroking her lower back and drawing her close for a prolonged kiss. "I've brought something special for us for dinner, and I thought we could...spend some *quality* time together?"

"Is *that* what you call it now?" she sighed. "Why does everything come at once, and not in the way that I'd hoped or planned?"

"Why? What's happened? Come, sit close to me...and...we'll... Oh! I'm sorry Sweetie, I can see now there really *is* something bothering you."

With her usual attention to detail Sophie explained what had taken place between herself and Julie. Her husband listened and frowned.

"Do you think I said the wrong thing?" she asked, anxiously.

"Sounds to me as though you handled yourself perfectly," he smiled, "particularly as I've found you quite composed, not curled up in bed crying as you used to do. I am so proud of you, Sweetie! Although I'm also concerned."

"Why?"

"Because when I went shopping for what I hoped would be our amorous evening meal I saw Julie's mother in the High Street; in fact I spoke with her... she was perfectly fine just a couple of hours ago."

"So Julie was not telling the truth; no wonder she got very irritated with me... you're never angry for the reason you think..."

"What?"

"Oh, just something I learned from Vanessa."

"You've learned a lot from being part of that group; I've not mentioned it before but really I'm so pleased; they seem to have helped you find yourself.

Now, do you think I ought to go to Julie's? He's sure to be at home and maybe I can find out what their emergency really is?" he suggested.

"No. I think I should go, then it won't seem as though we've discussed her. You stay home and have the amorous meal ready for when I return!"

"Wow! You are strong and determined, but don't you think it might be a good idea to... sort of... talk to Julie inside your head...before you go?"

"Where did that idea come from?"

"Umm... from Vanessa... I visited her at her home a little while ago."

"You did *what*? Why didn't you tell me? She never said..."

"Well, she wouldn't would she? Actually, Sweetie, she and I worked together about my little problem..."

"And this evening it doesn't seem as though you have a 'problem' at all… on this of all evenings! Anyway, I'm also feeling self-assured, so I'll visit Julie and I'll be back in an hour."

Julie's husband did not seem surprised as he opened the door to Sophie, "Come in," he said, sombrely, "she's upstairs on the bed. We had an almighty row last night; it was so intense that she said she wouldn't be here if I chose to come home from work today. Fancy saying that! She said she'd prefer to stay at her Mother's, but thankfully Mother-in-law supports me and told her to come back to her proper home with me and the kids."

"What did you row about?" Sophie asked, boldly.

"You, mainly."

"*Me?* I'd really like to know what I've done wrong."

"That's the point, dear Sophie, you've done nothing wrong. Surely you didn't think I was unaware that she's cut you off? I may be a man but I'm not insensitive - especially to the wiles of some women! For some reason last night I decided I'd had enough, so I faced her with her inexplicable behaviour towards you, told her that I expected her to come up with a good reason for ruining a perfectly good friendship between the four of us, and suggested we invite ourselves round to your home to apologise and make up."

"And she wouldn't?"

"She said something about how you'd got your own group of friends now, so you don't need her."

"It's the problem of the dough-nut hole," said Sophie, thoughtfully.

"It's what?" he asked.

"Something that I learned with my 'new' friends; it sounds silly, but the image makes perfect sense; there are things that I have recently discovered about myself that definitely gave me the courage to come and see you two this evening."

"I'm really glad to see you; would it be unreasonable for you just to give me a hug before you go and talk with her? Really, I'm beside myself with unhappiness, and actually prayed for someone to come and help me."

Sophie smiled to herself as she calmly walked upstairs. She knocked on Julie's bedroom door, walked in and sat on the bed beside the curled up heap of her "former" friend. She took hold of Julie's hand, brushed hair away from her eyes and for a second recalled how, just the previous day, the two of them had "talked" as though they were mother and daughter.

"Come on, Julie, take some deep breaths, drink your water and give me a hug."

Julie held Sophie close for a long while without speaking; and eventually she began to cry while hardly making a sound. Sophie waited until the tears subsided and then suggested, "Perhaps now you're ready to go downstairs? He's waiting for you, desperate to forgive you."

"Do you forgive me?" she asked, sounding like a frightened little girl.

"Of course I do, and if you like we can re-build our friendship, though not in the way it used to be; you see, I'm the same Sophie, but in the most remarkable way I've discovered what I am *really* like inside. I feel stronger, calmer and much happier than I ever could have imagined."

"I can feel the difference: you seem, well, *lighter*."

"Thank you; of all the helpful things you have said to me over the years, that is by far the nicest and most significant: I am lighter and I feel whole."

Julie frowned quizzically as they made their way downstairs where they were greeted by a very relieved husband, "Staying for a cuppa, Soph?"

"No thanks, I've got something special to do at home.

I'll talk with you tomorrow Julie?"

"Yes. Talk with you tomorrow."

On her way home Sophie found a place to stop; she pondered upon the way she and Julie, together with their husbands, apparently spontaneously and yet with easy simplicity, had rescued the breakdown of their friendship; she recalled Julie's husband's comment that he'd actually prayed for someone to come and help him, and she wondered: had his "prayer" been raised the previous evening just as she and Vanessa had been addressing the issue? Was this a wonderful result of the connectivity of thought that Vanessa had spoken of?

She hugged herself with delight as she realised that she had felt completely at ease while she had resolved an emotional problem with calm sensitivity; she knew she had discovered the meaning of loving empowerment that the Sputnik group had hoped to find in themselves; she gazed at the sky, lifted her arms above her head and breathed deeply in the cool evening air, "Thank you," she whispered, "Whoever you are, whatever you are, from the bottom of my heart, thank you for my wholeness."

Her meal and her husband were ready and waiting when she arrived home.

"Well?" he asked.

"I think those two will be doing now what I expect to do with you after we've eaten," she murmured, seductively.

"Sure you want to eat? Because I'm feeling ravenous."

"Let's eat later then," she said, with a mischievous smile.

And he followed her upstairs.

He felt satisfied and grateful.

Sophie leaned her head back against her pillow and sighed, "You know, I have a distinct feeling that right now we are expecting another baby."

"Oh, Sweetie, I think so too; perhaps we're also becoming intuitive? If it's a girl, do you think we should call her Vanessa?!"

Chapter 15   Principles

Maria's new challenge was how to fit everything into her day; she was used to hard work and for years had easily managed shift work along with organising her home; and then effortlessly she had taken on her substantial commitments at Sputnik's Hub, but now she felt that something more was demanding her attention.

"I've lots to do, and sumhow there was always time to fit it all in, but now I'm not so sure," she chattered to her "hubby", "yer don't mind do yer?"

"Yer know how I feel," he responded, "I'm 'appy if your 'appy.   Yer are aren't yer?   And yer seem to be managin' the kids better."

"It's not just me who should be lookin' after them yer know…it took two…"

"I know, I know, but yer doin' such a grand job," he grinned, as he settled in front of the television.

"I could be a bit more 'appy if I knew what's goin' on with me," she murmured, "so tonight I'm off for a talk with Vanessa, all right?"

Already fully absorbed in his armchair sport, he lazily waved his arm as she left.

Vanessa watched for Maria's approach from her living room window; she was uncharacteristically concerned as she wondered if her visitor would arrive as planned.   Her anxiety was not for the safety of the woman walking alone, her concern was whether Maria would actually turn up for their talk about healing because she knew that it was challenging for a person, already wary of their emerging skill, to fully embrace their healing ability.

So she was pleased to spot Maria in the distance and relieved to see her joyful wave as she approached the cottage: her childlike enthusiasm and unaffected greeting were refreshing.

"I'm glad to 'ave got 'ere," she beamed, "I thought one of my lads would decide he was still 'ungry and keep me cookin' all night, but Laura's kids have taken over my kitchen with Stevie, so I'll soon not have to worry about feedin' them at all!

Hello, Laura, I 'ope I'm not too noisy for yer!"

She hugged Laura and Vanessa with an enthusiasm that others lacked: she showed little fear of Laura's potential fragility and was always jovial with Vanessa, although on this occasion she appeared somewhat awed by the meeting as she and Vanessa settled in the living room while Laura went upstairs to rest.

"I could be a bit more 'appy if I knew what was goin' on with me," she repeated her gnawing concern. "But you'll 'elp me with it, won't yer?"

"That's what we're going to do this evening," Vanessa assured her. "You and I will chat for as long as you like about what it means to be a healer.

It's good that you have shared your concerns about 'what's going on with you' because the discovery of your

193

skill is bound to be troubling until you have grasped the meaning of the work."

"It's extra work that I'm worrid about. I've enough to do with my shifts, 'im at 'ome, and the kids, and now there's all the other stuff goin' on with us Sputniks. It's as much as I can 'andle; but the trouble is, when I tell myself 'no' to healin' I get sort of upset inside. It feels like I should give up everythin' else just to try and 'elp by healin', but I can't do that, I can't give up my kids, and I 'ave to earn a livin'."

"My dear Maria, there's no need to even consider giving up your home, your work, or even your devotion to the Sputnik group, for that matter. I believe you have the ability to be a gifted healer, and I'm sure you'll be able to do all that you feel is necessary for others without giving substantially more time and effort to the task."

"Well, I'll 'ave to work at it and I'll 'ave to try 'ard."

"I don't think so."

"How will I do a good job then?"

"You'll do a good job, as you put it, by simply bringing people into your thought during your meditation."

Maria smiled with relief: "I always 'ave time to meditate – everyday, no matter what, because I'm un'appy if I don't."

"Maria, I'm so delighted: you've really discovered yourself!"

"Don't know what you mean, Vanessa. I just meditate when I wake-up and then before I go to sleep, that's what keeps me 'appy. Sumtimes I meditate quite well, and then sumtimes it feels like I'll never get my mind to be quiet."

"That problem applies to us all; the answer is to be patient with yourself and persevere with the practice, and especially: try not to try!"

"I've bin tryin' all my life! But my big problem is I'm not as 'appy now as when I started all this stuff, and I want to know why."

"You've already experienced what it's like to spontaneously react to the inner need to heal when you were faced with Colin's unhappy dog; you've continued to respond to your natural ability in Sputnik's kitchen by preparing exactly what we all need to eat; you've done well finding out about chakras and healing energy, and you've freely explored and accepted the unusual things you see around you – in fact I was thrilled at the way you explained some metaphysical ideas to the group."

"But, as I said, Vanessa, I'm still not 'appy with it all; it feels like there's sumthin' else I should be doin'"

"And your disquiet tells us both that you are ready to learn more about the art of healing," said Vanessa, gently. "I'll make some tea and we'll talk for a while, and then perhaps I'll invite Laura to come down and join us."

Maria followed Vanessa into the kitchen to help prepare their drinks, and while Vanessa carried a tray to Laura she inquisitively looked around the sitting room.

"I like it 'ere," she remarked when Vanessa returned, "it's very... nice."

"So people say!" Vanessa smiled. "Now where were we?"

"You were explainin' what's goin' on with me. P'raps it's the way I feel around people?"

"How *do* you feel?"

"Sumtimes angry, and if I'm not angry, then I'm sad."

"Why do you suppose you have these feelings?"

"Because they keep things to themselves."

"What sort of things?"

"Well, yer know, people don't say what they mean, they pretend about 'most everythin': they don't say how they really feel, they say nice things while they're thinkin' sumthink 'orrible, and they pretend everythin' is fine when it really isn't."

"It's the way of the world, Maria: most people are not as authentic as you, and your discomfort around them is because you are seeing right through their inauthenticity; often you feel what they truly feel; in fact you are firmly connected to their heart and soul."

"Umm…whatever it is, it's gettin' worse: ever since Colin's dog the feelin's have bin gettin' worse."

Vanessa moved to the sofa to sit close to Maria.

"Would you have preferred the experience not to have happened?"

"No, I'm glad it did. It felt good to 'elp the dog, and I've been sendin' my thoughts to Colin so I've bin 'elping him too, and most of all it's bin fantastic to find out all the amazin' things about what food everyone needs. I know when their bodies are feelin' better!"

"How do you know that?"

"Well, if their body is feelin' sick, or not right, I want to put my hand near them or give them sumthin' different to eat; and when I don't want to do anythin' for them, or when I feel sort of calm near them, then I know they're all right."

Vanessa rubbed her forehead and leaned forward in thoughtful concern: she knew well the challenge Maria faced to find satisfaction in an illusory world, "My dear, I hope that during this evening you will learn some important principles which will keep you happy in your work."

"I want to learn everythin' so that people 'round me are 'appy, then I'm 'appy – just like my hubby says!" she beamed.

"That's a truly wonderful way to be, but unfortunately it's not very healthy for *you*."

"I need to think about me first and stop worryin' about havin' lots to do?"

"Indeed you do. In fact that is the first, and most important, of a few ideas that I'd like to share with you so that in future you will not be overwhelmed by work and not feel disturbed about your feelings or worried about how to help others.

My second suggestion is that you should be sure to meditate – and you've already told me how important that practice is to you; it keeps you happy because it keeps you in touch with your spirit.

The third piece of advice is to make sure that you care for your body: find ways to be in touch with every aspect of it so that you know all is well."

"I already do that in the shower or when I'm in bed: I start at my feet and sort of talk to each bit of my body right up to my 'ead; sumhow I know when sumthink's not right and I ask myself what it could be."

"What answers do you receive?"

"I find out if there's anger stuck in my gut, or worry makin' my neck ache; then I think about when I was angry or why I was worrid and I try to think of a better way of feelin' so I don't get poorly."

"Exactly. You understand that the way you think and feel influences the health of your body."

"What else must I do so that I feel 'appy with healin'?"

"I think it's important that when you are asked to help others you should suggest only things that you have already explored for yourself."

"Like with our kids: me and my hubby tell 'em things that we know work for us."

"That's the way of good parents. And perhaps you've also seen how your children have things to teach you?"

"I dunno; but me and my hubby say that when the kids are doin' sumthin' that really makes us mad, it's because we've done those things ourselves, and we don't want them to make the same mistakes…

That's made me think: I came in 'ere moaning to you about how I feel sad when people are pretendin'... Well, I'm pretendin' arnt I?"

"About what, Maria?"

"I'm tryin' to pretend that I don't do healin'... and it makes me feel worse inside: that's what's goin' on with me!"

"Is that so?"

There was an uncharacteristic pause in Maria's chatter as she thought through their hectic discussion, and then she slowly inquired:

"Vanessa, when you say, 'Is that so?' you're tellin' me I'm gettin' the hang of things aren't yer?"

"Is that so?" Vanessa raised her eyebrows playfully, and then continued more seriously, "Maria, I want you to understand that it's not easy being a healer: your head wants you to be normal – to be like other people and fit in with the world, but when you follow your head you realise that you're betraying yourself by turning your back on your ability; this makes you feel unhappy and may cause you to become ill.

Your skill was awakened when you worked with Colin's dog, your spirit would like you to continue doing its work, and you become upset when you choose not to do so."

Maria nodded; she moved to sit opposite her teacher; her wide eyes showed she'd become engrossed in Vanessa's guidance:

"If you intend to follow your spirit's direction it is essential that you understand that it's not possible to fix everyone; indeed, it's not even appropriate to do so. Listen to your heart and learn to be discerning: to heal is not to make everything right, the aim is to help others find their inner self so that they realise who they really are.

It's important that you allow others to make their own choices; and you should try not to become anxious or angry when others choose not to listen to their heart. In other words, if people choose to pretend, allow them to do so because that is part of the adventure of their life."

Maria rested her chin on her cupped hands and silently absorbed the wisdom:

"I think that each time you greet a person you'll find it meaningful to address them with the word, *Namaste*, meaning: 'the true spirit that is me, greets the true spirit that is you.' When you say this to others – even if you simply whisper it inside your head - you will be acknowledging their true self, even if they continue to choose not to behave as their spirit wishes.

Once you have spoken 'Namaste' you will have done something for them spiritually – you will have spoken to their heart, so you can happily move on, free from the burden of thinking that there might be more for you to do."

"So I'll be 'appy when I agree with my heart that I should do healin'; and to make sure I'm a good healer I need to meditate and look after myself, then I can 'elp others; but I mustn't mind if they're not interested, and I shouldn't expect that my job is to fix everythin'."

"You seem to have summed up our discussion very well," said Vanessa.

"Is that so?" Maria grinned.

Laura tapped on the living room door, "I was wondering if it's appropriate for me to join you?"

"Indeed it is," said Vanessa. "Maria, I was hoping that you and Laura might spend a little time together to share your experiences of healing. We're not anticipating that any work needs to be done for Laura because she's already happy with her plan of complementary health: she combines the skill of her physician with a wealth of alternative practices - including a personal healer! But it may be valuable for you both to share impressions of that work."

"Yes," said Laura, "I'll sit quietly, perhaps with my eyes closed, while you tell me what you think and feel."

Maria cleared her throat and nervously responded, "If you don't mind, I need to go and wash my hands first... I'm not goin' to touch you Laura, but it's sumthin' I have to do."

Vanessa smiled her approval, "It's the ritual of cleansing before coming into close contact with another's energy," she explained.

"Oh, I didn't know, I just thought it was a bit more of my weirdness!"

When she returned, Maria stood back and surveyed Laura's resting figure. Then she closed her eyes and commented:

"Dear Laura, I was very sad when Frank told us how poorly yer were and I desperately wanted to make yer better. But Vanessa explained how it was best to just think about yer from my heart. That's what I've bin doin' every day... we all have. And now we're so 'appy that you're back. We think you're brave and strong.

I feel how strong you are: there's wonderful purple and green round yer heart, and turquoise blue runs like a river from yer heart to the places where it's needed – yer breasts and tummy. Those places seem red to me, they're hot because of the healin' that Vanessa has bin doin' for you, and her heart has bin working with your heart so yer can keep healin' yourself. That's what I think."

"I'm sure Laura welcomes your healing love," Vanessa murmured.

Laura nodded.

"My healin' love looks like white light that shines out of my heart to Laura's, and it shines to you too Vanessa, thank you for 'elpin' me."

"May I also receive from you?" Frank spoke from the corner of the room where he'd silently watched and waited. "I've been here a few minutes and I'm grateful to have witnessed the beautiful sight of dear Maria talking of the wonder of my wife's healing." He moved towards them and gave each a prolonged hug, "Laura and I are so grateful for the many ways you two have supported and healed us."

"Actually, it's been the one joy of my illness," said Laura, "perhaps even the reason for it: that we are here this evening having discovered unusual togetherness through the Sputnik group.

And yes, as Frank has said, we are so very grateful to you."

"And we are privileged to witness the courage and love of you both," said Vanessa. "Now, Maria and I will leave you to have time together while she and I walk to the village."

The evening was still and the moon brightened their path as they walked.

"Ain't life wonderful?"

"It is; absolutely wonderful.

Tell me Maria, was there a time in your life when you thought that life was not wonderful?"

"Aw, Vanessa, I 'ad a very bad start to life...really bad. But that's all behind me now, ever since me and my 'ubby met... We were very young when we got together, but we were good for each other, right from the start. He 'ad a tough up-bringin', but he's kind to me and the kids, and he works 'ard... in fact...we luv each other...a lot."

"Perhaps your 'bad start to life' and your subsequent emerging happiness taught you some significant things about the world? I'm thinking that perhaps your reaction to life's tough journey is one reason why you're so in touch with your spirit?"

"I've never really thought about it; life 'as its ups and downs."

"It does, Maria, but as you have found, the way we come through the 'downs' makes us stronger and more perceptive to the needs of others."

"You think that's a reason why I'm discoverin' this stuff about healin'?"

"I do. And I think as your life unfolds you will teach many people what it means to embrace life's ups and downs...that is, if you choose to do so."

Maria was suddenly distracted from her moment of serious contemplation:

"Look! Would yer believe it! There's a light on in the school – in the 'ead-teacher's office. He ought to have finished by now; he should be at 'ome."

"Indeed he should."

"Yer know, Colin and Frank keep sayin' the problem is about his daughter... but that's not what I think..."

"Is that so?" Vanessa replied. "Well, I've walked far enough for this evening, shall we say goodbye here?"

They hugged briefly and Vanessa murmured, "Stick to your principles, Maria – I know you will!"

"Namaste, Vanessa: my heart speaks to yours!"

For a while Vanessa waited by the school gate; and then, as the moon slipped behind gathering clouds and the sky darkened, she frowned and carefully made her way home by torchlight.

Chapter 16 Disclosure

Malcolm had not attended Sputnik's Hub meetings for some time; the others had seen him in school but he avoided opportunities to talk with them. It was generally accepted that he no longer wanted to be part of the group, especially since he'd obviously had difficulty staying in the room when their deliberations apparently bothered him.

However, the "Sputniks" were unaware that he was another of their group who had been grateful to meet Vanessa at home where she continued to help him with specific challenges.

Throughout his career he had always been committed to providing his pupils with the best possible learning opportunities, and it occurred to him that the community's positive attitude towards the Sputnik group could help him formulate new aims for the school, so he became seriously absorbed with ideas for improving the school's ethos far beyond what was generally considered good practice.

He had been satisfied that after years of wise leadership and dedication his school was clearly focussed upon enthusiasm for learning and respect for others, but he realised that its environment would be enriched by the introduction of strategies suggested by Vanessa, and gradually he came to the conclusion that he should bring her ideas to the attention of the teachers and governors.

His plan was to slowly educate the most amenable colleagues and also to explore the ideas in the classroom himself, but he was surprised when he discovered that much of Vanessa's teaching was already well understood by many children: it was as if mushrooms of wisdom had been sprouting around him without his knowledge. His lack of information about what was already blossoming in the classrooms concerned him because he had always been proud of his awareness of both progress and problems in his school.

He had studied Colin's "mission statements" with the intention of adapting them for children's understanding, but his difficulties made him seek Vanessa's help:

"Let me go over again what our school already achieves so that my mind can formulate what our future goals should be," he began. "Although, Vanessa, I've come to the conclusion that some of our children are already ahead of me, and I suspect it's because of your influence when you work with them. How has that come about? What do you do with them? Is it some psychic phenomenon that I will never know - nor indeed want to know, especially in the precious environment of the school?"

"You know the answer to all of your questions," she replied. "Success in the classroom comes from the strategy that is well-known by good educators like yourself: Begin with what the children already know, set your goal of future attainment, plan a route of small steps toward that goal, and ensure that you have your teachers and parents with you on the journey. My philosophy is similar: always begin with yourself, be understanding of your situation, take small steps towards your goal and don't be distracted by psychic phenomena!"

He smiled and took hold of her hand, "You know I love you, Vanessa?"

"Yes, and as I've told you on many occasions, I know exactly how you feel," she replied, solemnly.

"Oh no, you've no idea how I feel!" he snapped, as he abruptly withdrew his hand. "Lately I've been losing touch with what's happening around me and I'm becoming unsure of things I say: Of course I don't love you…I'm married, have a teenage daughter…and you're…"

"Old enough to be your mother!" Her humour helped to dissolve his sudden agitation as she continued to explain her feelings, "Malcolm, the way I see it, there is nothing wrong with expressions of love: the emotion doesn't have to be construed as romance or passion, and neither should speaking of love necessarily cause feelings of betrayal."

"Oh, well, I think I knew that," he said, looking at the floor with embarrassment.

Vanessa ignored his discomfort and continued to clarify her point of view: "It's absurd how some people avoid the word 'Dear' when they write letters these days because they think it signifies an emotional attachment; and some recipients of my mail are uneasy when I end my message, 'Love, Vanessa'. They have no idea that I really do Love them in the most heart-felt sense possible, so why should I not say so?"

"Yes, yes, I hear you!" he said, hiding his humiliation behind his witty response: "And so our first teaching objective must be to have all the children understand how to use 'yours faithfully' and 'yours sincerely' correctly... Dear Vanessa!

Seriously, though, I need to formulate a strategy of presenting your philosophy to our teachers: I need to create a plan for a day-long presentation and open discussion so that the concepts may be formally introduced throughout the school; it is also imperative that I create an opportunity to talk to parents about the ideas; so do you have time to work with me?"

Their preparation took weeks of deliberation; they worked together and occasionally invited individuals and small groups from the school and wider community to debate their ideas. Gradually, as the subject became more widely discussed, Malcolm assured his staff that their attendance at the planned meeting would be voluntary:

"This is unlike most educational training," he explained, "it's a way of life, and therefore it's inappropriate, indeed impossible, for me to impose it upon any of you. However, I'm sure you will have noticed how some of these ideas have already made a positive change to the attitudes and behaviour of our children. "

As his plans took shape, Malcolm was relieved that all colleagues – some through genuine interest, others with scepticism – indicated that they would take part in the day's seminar which he described as: "An explanation and discussion of the ethos of the Sputnik group with ideas of how it may be applied to our school." He was also delighted with the positive response of many parents which meant that a larger than expected audience was anticipated, and so a meeting in the school hall was planned rather than a gathering at Sputnik's Hub.

Having perfected his strategy Malcolm felt relief from the weight of initial planning and eventually reappeared at Sputnik's Hub where his explanation of being overwhelmed by his project was accepted as the reason for his absence.

He took time to present his proposals, and then surprised the group by asking for their help:

"It's like this," he said cautiously, "I would like some of you to speak during the presentation day; I believe that under the umbrella of Vanessa's philosophy we have all gained particular knowledge – we've specialised, if you like; and let's be honest, no one wants to listen to me speak for the whole day!

So I was hoping that each of you might choose something that you would like to talk about to help the audience understand the ethos behind us Sputniks, and hopefully we will engage the adults so that they actively participate in the plan to develop our children's awareness of themselves."

"Speak to a crowded hall you mean?" asked Gabby, incredulously.

"Not me," said Maria, "I don't know anythin' worth talkin' about."

"Indeed you do," said Colin, "even if we disregard your obvious abilities at Vanessa's side, you are an expert at choosing appropriate food for us all."

"I second that," said Frank. "You could talk to the people in the hall just like you do when you're preparing our meals; you could explain what we should eat and describe the positive effect of certain foods on our body; I don't know where you get all the information, but the food – and your conversation - satisfies us all!"

"I don't know where I get the ideas from either," muttered Maria, "but I s'pose I should tell more people what I think."

"That's settled then."

"And I suppose I could talk about how it's possible to communicate with infants using inner perception," said Sophie, shyly. "The methods I've been trying out with my own children have been well received by some other mothers when I've had the opportunity to explain and practice with them...though our conversations have only been between two or three of us in our homes... It will be rather different talking to a large audience ..."

"I'm sure you'll do really well; thank you for your proposal," Malcolm interrupted briskly, "and I'll follow your explanation by offering suggestions for older children."

"That leaves me talking about inspiring the adolescents!" Frank muttered.

"Perhaps I might talk about how our learning affects our attitude to ourselves and our home," suggested Gabby. "I mean, I'd not talk about how my home life used to be, but how it is now. But I'm like Sophie: we've both been getting on rather well sharing our ideas with other women in their homes, but I have the same reluctance about speaking to an audience…though if others are willing to try, I will too."

"I've heard of your popularity and success in the community," said Vanessa warmly, "you've both been marvellous ambassadors for the Sputnik group, and I suspect that by reaching out to others you have contributed to the success of the 'Lunch 'n Lectures'.

So, that leaves Colin and me to work on something together in support of Malcolm's presentation day."

"Well, I'd like to be chairman, since I've had that kind of experience," said Colin, decisively, "and you, Vanessa, ought to be free to answer questions and step in whenever we hesitate."

"Thank you all for your willingness, although I'm aware I've virtually forced you into helping me!" Malcolm confessed. "I'll try to make the day as informal as possible: I'm not expecting you to stand up and make a speech; we'll all sit together and talk about our skills, our practices and experiences - just as we do in this room."

The group gained inspiration from each other and soon became enthusiastic about the project so that when they came together to agree details they were more certain of how to present their ideas.

Malcolm started them off. "I'll talk about a plan to introduce a few moments of whole class stillness each day; we'll use different methods depending upon the age of the children: Infants might be guided to imagine colours in and around themselves; middle years might become attentive to their breathing, just for a minute or so; and the older children may discover a phrase or mantra that helps to improve their ability to be still.

Our school staff will also be encouraged to create opportunities for children to promote their self-respect - not necessarily from good behaviour, perseverance and excellent work - but through an ethos of 'no matter what... you are respected.'

These gentle ideas are a start, and we will review the children's reaction and behaviour during our usual staff meetings; in fact, the children themselves will be encouraged to review their own progress of self-respect."

Sophie looked thoughtful: "I ought to have the courage to speak before you, Malcolm, so that the ideas for babies and toddlers are presented first: that way we'd show parents that our thinking has a sense of progression.

I'll talk about my experience of having my baby daughter on my knee – as Vanessa showed us months ago. I've been practicing with her for a few moments every day.

Also, I've been discovering how it's possible to bond with both my children simply by thinking: like Vanessa, I close my eyes for a time of stillness, and then I imagine a discussion in my head with each of them: I remind them that I love them – no matter what," she smiled at Malcolm, "and then I continue as if I am having quite a mature conversation with them about themselves, the world and their place in it.

I believe it has made my daughter much calmer, my son seems more self-assured and has become quite responsive to the needs of others, and I feel closer to them both."

"I use the same phrase – 'no matter what' - with the youth group," said Frank. "They appear to be responding to the idea that their adolescent revolutions are accepted, especially when they create responsible ways of expressing their moods, feelings and ideas.

The plan with them is to stretch their credulity about the world and their place in it, and we hope to accept their alternative views without judging them…or have them judge adults and authority.

Eventually we may be successful in showing them ways to look inward, to become self-watchers, so that they begin to understand the reasons for their own behaviour and that of their peers.

Some of them may take meditation seriously.

Like Malcolm and his staff, the idea is that we will review progress together, keep a record of what we achieve, and involve the kids with future plans."

"I'm plannin' on visitin' the youth group to talk about food," said Maria. "Shouldn't think they'd like the idea of talkin' to their body to find out what it needs, but the younger kids know how to do that already; Stevie brings different friends to the house...can you believe it? There are children in other classes who want to be his friend now!

Anyhow, the youngest ones are very good at followin' my idea: They stand in the middle of the kitchen and 'dream' what they think they should eat; you'd be surprised what they decide...sumtimes even broccoli!

Sumhow, I need to find a way of explainin' this to their mums and dads, and I was thinkin' of usin' Malcolm as an example," she added, mischievously.

"An example of what?" Malcolm looked mildly alarmed.

"Haven't yer noticed what yer own body wants?" she asked.

"Err, such as?" he asked, nervously.

Maria sighed, "Yer such a clever man but yer don't pay attention to things that are important for yerself: You've been askin' me for weeks if it's possible for me to serve breakfasts; yer said yer had a taste for porridge. Then yer badgered me for some of my flapjack biscuits, and yer wanted some oat mix with yer lunch-time dessert...Don't that tell yer sumthin' about yer body?"

"I'm not sure what you're getting at," he responded, his tension rising.

215

"Yer body is tellin' yer it needs oats," she almost shouted. "So yer might have high blood pressure, and eatin' oats will help yer feel better."

Malcolm coughed, shifted in his chair and fidgeted with his shirt collar, but as Gabby joined in their discussion he was distracted from his discomfort by her concerns: "I don't know how to follow all these ideas," she grumbled, "you all have a clear plan and I'm afraid I'll just clam up and look silly."

"Remember, we're all here to help each other," said Malcolm, finally recovering from Maria's onslaught. "Perhaps we'll ask you how you arrange colour schemes in your home, how you create places where you can be quiet and thoughtful, or how you add to spaces to make them appealing; our questions will help you to talk about your new-found skill."

"You'll easily be able to share your ideas with our audience," said Sophie. "Just imagine you are talking to me - like the time when you explained how you've learned to be less anxious with your daughter and grand-daughter. You know, you often remind me to use our 'remember yourself' mantra when I obsess about what other people think of me. So I'm sure you'll be an inspiration to others, just as you are for me."

Gabby reached over to hug her young friend, "Alright, thank you for your encouragement. But please remember, I'm the one who needs your guidance and support. Don't you dare leave me looking dumb!"

"We have every confidence that you will have lots to say!" Malcolm nudged her playfully. "And, by the way, I've also been thinking that we should create intervals during the day to demonstrate the various methods we use to meditate. In fact, if meditation is the only thing our listeners grasp, then the day will have been truly worthwhile!"

The presentation day meant that the school was closed, though the building came alive with the buzz of people from the community who wanted to learn alongside their school teachers.

As Maria watched the crowd's arrival from the safety of Sputnik's Hub she grew less concerned about her impending talk: "I'm more worrid about how many people will come 'ere for lunch," she muttered.

"It'll be like feeding the five thousand," joked Frank. "Tell us how you decided upon the menu," he added, knowing that conversation would ease her anxiety.

"I close my eyes..."

"Seriously? You close your eyes?" said Malcolm, mischievously.

"Yes, I close my eyes, like Vanessa does when she wants to concentrate; then I sort of talk to my body and their bodies and ask what they would like to eat."

"And they talk back to you!"

"Now, Malcolm, I know you're trying to lessen the anxiety about our day, but you are in danger of sounding like our worst critics," said Vanessa, "and they may be sitting in the hall waiting for us in just that kind of mood."

"Sorry. Sorry Maria. I really was trying to lighten up; I feel anxious myself, even though I'm used to talking to large groups. Vanessa, please show us how you have taught me to prepare for public speaking."

She nodded. "Make yourself comfortable; rest your spine against the back of your chair and place your feet firmly on the floor.

Focus your attention upon your breathing: notice your breath in... and out; in... and out; be aware of the rise and fall of your abdomen as you breathe in and out.

When thoughts come into your mind let them drift away like clouds across an expansive blue sky; and when you feel ready, repeat our mantra quietly, under your breath:
Remember your SELF
RE-member your Self
Remember YOURSELF"

When the group had relaxed into the procedure she continued, "Imagine a wave of orange which enters your toes and your feet, and rises up your legs.

As you continue to breathe, the orange seeps into your hips and rises through your abdomen; it suffuses your heart and from there it flows from your mouth; it saturates your head and pours out from your forehead.

You are a fount of orange.

Picture yourself seated in front of today's audience and notice how your tide of orange pours from you and reaches the people in front of you: orange suffuses your listeners; they are attentive to your heart; they gaze at you with love and awe and the tide of orange floats from them back to you."

She paused to allow them to assimilate the process, and then she said briskly, "Alright, allow this process to continue, and as you take some deep breaths bring yourself to full consciousness in anticipation of an enjoyable day.

Now, let's go and greet our guests!"

The response of the audience to Malcolm's strong and engaging welcome showed that he had the confidence and support of school staff and parents. His natural ability to speak with clarity and humour, together with compassion and patient understanding, meant that even when he and others faced searching questions, his self-assured presence brought speakers and listeners together in an atmosphere of mutual support and empathy. Their original plan to have Vanessa in the role of intermediary was unnecessary: she remained silent throughout the day, though the Sputniks knew that her thoughtful presence was touching them all.

As the day's discussions came to a close, and after their audience had departed, the Sputniks withdrew to the Hub, elated and satisfied with their successful presentation.

"Congratulations everyone," said Vanessa. "I've heard Colin say: 'we teach what we need to learn' and today you created wonderful moments, teaching others what you wanted to learn yourselves. I am sure you have surpassed your own expectations of how much you understand metaphysics."

"Though, if it wasn't for you, Vanessa, we wouldn't have known how to access this inner wisdom," said Colin.

"And if Sophie hadn't been crying outside school, we wouldn't have come together and created Sputnik's Hub," added Gabby, triumphantly. "Oh Malcolm, I'm so glad you came out to us that day. Thank you for giving us the freedom to use this room," she hugged him tightly, and then, somewhat embarrassed, she drew back. "Oh no! Look, I'm so sorry; I've left make-up on your crisp white shirt; I'm sure it will stain. Whatever will your wife say?"

"She won't say anything because she won't know; and even if she saw the smudge she wouldn't care," said Malcolm.

"Wouldn't *care*?"

"No, she wouldn't care; and I can't blame her."

"Why Malcolm, what's happened between you?"

"Have you argued about your daughter's behaviour?"

"You do know that arguments are quite normal in families dealing with teenage problems?"

"I know. But in my family our daughter is not the problem. I am."

"Too much time spent at work?"

"Not that either, though I have buried myself in work to try and relieve my guilt."

"Guilt? About what?"

"Ok. It's time to tell you…" Malcolm took a deep breath, turned his face to the ceiling and closed his eyes: "My wife and I have split up…. actually…err… to be absolutely truthful… I've abandoned my wife… and my daughter… because…well… because I'm gay."

They fell silent.

Eventually Gabby voiced their astonishment with a nervous stammer: "But you're… married… you've got a daughter… a teenager… you told us…you were having difficulty…"

Drenched in misery, Malcolm bowed his head and stood motionless and submissive surrounded by the hesitant group.

Gabby moved away and Vanessa took her place by his side. Once again he fell into her arms and sobbed, "I can't help it…I couldn't help it… we met at a conference… I had to tell my wife… I've betrayed her…lost any respect my daughter had for me…left my home… And now that I've come out I'll lose my job…my career…and the respect of the community… But that hardly matters because my self-respect is in shreds… I just can't help the way I feel…"

"Don't see why you'll lose your job," muttered Maria, seriously, "it's not as if we're gonna complain to the council."

Sophie and Gabby suppressed their smiles – their reaction was not a sign of embarrassment, but a shared acknowledgement of how far they had all come as fellow travellers on life's journey.

Chapter 17 Walk the Talk

Vanessa wrapped her arms firmly around Malcolm, "Don't run," she whispered, "Do not run. Stand firm and strong while we allow and accept... allow and accept... allow and accept."

Malcolm's breathing calmed and his body relaxed; he slumped into a chair, and with head bowed he sighed, "Ok, my friends, for once I'll not run away. Do what you want with me, I'm ready."

"We're not about to judge you, Malcolm," said Frank. "And every one of us here knows what it means to be trustworthy, particularly when we're in this room: it was our solemn agreement.

What you choose to say about coming out, and how the authorities react to you, is between you and them. For me, I stand by you. Your outstanding ability as a teacher and head-teacher is unquestioned in this community. Laura and I have trusted our children to your care. Our trust and our appreciation of you and your work will continue."

"What you do outside school is not anyone else's business, though I must say I feel for your wife," said Gabby bluntly.

"I'm upset because of the way Malcolm feels about himself," said Sophie. "How may we help you? Please let us do whatever we can for you." She knelt by his side and looked up at Vanessa: "Please guide us through this; we must help him."

Colin moved away from the group to the corner of the room where he apparently needed to attend to his dog, "Well, I never...well, I never..." he muttered.

"What are your thoughts, Maria?" Vanessa asked.

"Well, for a long time we've bin tryin' to keep up with Malcolm: we respected him when he said we should all be askin', 'Who am I?'. He thought the idea was important, so we thought it must be too. We've bin usin' the mantra hopin' it would 'elp us change the way we think about ourselves and others: we've bin tryin' to learn how to love each other - no matter what. So now it's time for us to walk our talk," she said, innocently.

"Walk our talk...you're right... Let's think... We have our 'mission statement' pinned to the wall... You know, Colin, the one you produced a few months ago? Perhaps we should have it here on the table in front of us?" Vanessa suggested.

Frank brought the paper to the table as Colin rushed across the room, "Don't use this, Vanessa; I don't want my thoughts to be the topic of *this* discussion," he whispered, fiercely.

"Shhh, what do you mean?" Maria scolded him, "Don't take this so hard."

"I believed in him, I was a member of the board who appointed him as head-teacher of our school. We all have our secrets, but this..." he hissed.

"I don't know what's got into you, Colin. You were angry when Frank was strugglin' with Laura's illness, and you were so cross when Malcolm kept leavin' our meetings; now at least you can be glad that Laura is recoverin', and at last you can see what's bin hurting Malcolm."

"Recovering? Hurting? What about *me*?" Colin's screech was loud enough for them all to hear.

"*You* are very much needed right here to read your affirmations to us." Vanessa's tone was like that of a school matron exercising her discipline. "Come, Colin," she said, more gently, "you worked so hard to produce these statements, and now we need you to read them to us so that we can go away and decide what it really means to 'walk our talk'.

Then, at our next meeting, I suggest we use your statements as our discussion agenda."

"That's a good idea," said Frank. "These clever, but simple, sentences will guide our thoughts towards a deeper understanding of ourselves; and surely Colin, that's just what you had in mind."

"I'm not sure I want to discuss what's on my mind," Colin replied, broodingly.

"Well, you'll feel much better by the time we all meet again," said Maria, cheerily, "Yer know I'll find sumthin' that's just right for your unsettled tummy, and my kids'll keep yer mind off whatever's botherin' yer!"

Weeks passed without any firm date being decided for their meeting, and during that time there was a change in circumstance for some Sputniks, while for a few, life continued as before: To the relief of most of the group the school remained under Malcolm's leadership; Laura grew strong enough to return home and gradually resumed most of her familiar responsibilities although Maria and her children were never far away from Laura and Frank's household, consequently the community noted a definite decline in incidents of petty crime and adolescent disturbance in the locality.

After Gabby's and Sophie's successful presentations the demand in the community for their skills grew: their plans for home re-styling and instructions for child-care based upon natural insight and inner wisdom became a business enterprise attached to the Sputnik organisation.

Colin's route for walks now took him to more solitary places; his discontent grew as he reflected upon how he had once dreamed of a potential relationship with Vanessa; he felt a sense of loathing, though occasionally he recognised that his dislike was more of himself than of her.

Vanessa and Malcolm continued to work together on their mission to spread the Sputnik ethos; they were particularly motivated by the positive response to the day's seminar and by the continued interest in lunch time meetings.

They believed that an evening event would be well received and took their time to mull over ideas to bring together the original Sputniks, their peripheral groups and the wider community.

Eventually they settled upon a plan for the presentation of their "Lore" - derived from Colin's original statements; and they anticipated that a guided discussion of the philosophy would help them all understand and affirm it.

Once again, they established their basic plan before introducing the idea to the rest of the group who then enthusiastically contributed more thoughts; Colin was secretly glad to be once more at the centre of activity, Malcolm was relieved that their response to him and his ideas had not changed from when he had led them in their first community outreach, and when Frank persuaded some of the youngsters to take part, they all looked forward to welcoming younger members to Sputnik's Hub accompanied by their interested parents.

As late spring brought warmer weather and light evenings, their event was eagerly anticipated. They had decided upon a seasonal gathering, a celebration of freedom and refreshment, to include a special meal and an opportunity for extended, thought-provoking discussion; and as if in welcome of the occasion, the evening sun shone as the curious and excited guests made their way to the school for the unusual event.

Maria had prepared a community meal of dishes that harmonized with the theme of freshness, cleansing and renewal, and she hoped that the hungry teenagers would welcome fruits and salads as a novel departure from their preferred diet.

The meal tables, tightly squeezed into Sputnik's Hub, were decorated with Gabby's choice of fabric and colour matching the summery freshness of the evening, and as the groups took their places their excited conversation was interrupted by Maria who called for their attention for her surprise announcement:

"Everyone. Listen. It's time for you to thank your chef – the young man who 'elped choose the menu for you this evenin'…" she beckoned from the kitchen door and proudly pushed Stevie to the centre of the room; red faced, he received the applause with surprising maturity, and then whispered something to his Mother.

"Oh," she said, "Stevie would like you to meet his number one 'elper – the person who chops the food and cleans the pans…" Stevie's Dad emerged from the kitchen: red faced like his youngest son, he was greeted by whistles and cheers from the rest of the brood and from Frank's children.

Malcolm left his place at the table and made his way to Maria; he shook her hand and raised his voice above the noise:

"Thanks Maria, thank you very much; you and your family have worked hard to prepare this evening's meal; we're looking forward to finding out what our body needs to maintain its good health!"

"Yer daft man, don't shake my hand, give me a hug,"
Maria commanded, as the cheers grew louder.

"Let's eat!"

After their meal Colin was pleased to assume his self-important role as chairman, but those in the audience who needed an explanation for the title of the evening's discussion waited in vain:

"We call it Sputnik's Lore," he announced, "though for the life of me I can't remember why!"

Enjoying their laughter, he explained, "I'll read each item of our lore and Vanessa will guide our thoughts."

Sputnik's Lore: Accepting Ourselves

"Your title is incredibly potent," Vanessa began. "Accepting - together with allowing and acknowledging - are states of heart to which we should aspire."

"You call them states of heart, rather than states of mind?" Colin queried.

"Well, the way I see it, our thought emerges from our heart space. We point at our heart when we refer to ourselves, and our interaction with others is heart focussed rather than head directed: It's from our heart that we acknowledge ourselves and others, and with our heart's intent we accept and allow whatever choices each of us makes."

We own our idiosyncrasies and personality traits which tend to make us anxious; our acceptance means we avoid saying: "I wish I was different."

"Does anyone have anything to say about this first statement?"

"I do." Gabby stood up. "This is so relevant to me; the practice of self-acceptance is very calming - when I remember to do it," she smiled. "When I admit what I'm like and give myself reassurance, or just shrug my shoulders, I find things go better for me. In the past, when I cried and moaned about my behaviour it just made things worse."

"Don't you think that it's a weakness to accept your difficulties?" asked Colin.

"It's the way that I accept them, that matters," said Gabby, "and that depends upon the situation. Sometimes I'm able to tell myself not to be so silly or so serious about an issue, and sometimes it's best for me to be gentle and self-loving; though there are still times when I allow myself to have a good cry, but afterwards I avoid blaming myself for my tears."

"Could you give us an example of what happens?" asked Vanessa.

"Easily. My daughter and I - she's here this evening – are working on improving the way we communicate. I'm learning to accept that I can be unreasonable when I want things to be perfect, and that I can be controlling and bossy sometimes when we talk. In a practical way we are both learning about the dynamics of our conversation and we are adapting the way we relate to each other.

However, it's during the night that my problem really takes hold: I spend ages thinking and reviewing what has been said during the day; I toss and turn, and then replay conversations in my mind to try to make them seem better. But since I've been part of the Sputnik group I've had success by gradually adapting my behaviour and accepting things I cannot change; so now at night I'm kind to myself as I gently remember that my repetitive thoughts are unnecessary, and I use relaxation techniques to get to sleep rather than creating ridiculous plans to try to be someone completely different."

"Thank you, Gabby. You're very brave telling us these things, and actually many of us could find similar issues in ourselves; it helps just to know that the difficulty is being experienced by someone else," said Colin, warmly.

We recognise that even though we possess these traits, it is possible for us to learn ways of reducing their impact and even be free of them completely.

"Vanessa has shown us the way here."

"Yes, thank you, Colin. There are several strands to heal our difficulties: First, as Gabby has explained, it is essential to accept a problem without becoming upset whenever it occurs; this is a huge step towards resolution. Then it's useful to learn personal ways to control and cope with any extreme reaction during moments of distress. Next, it is beneficial to seek therapeutic help to uncover the deep reason why the issue exists. And finally it is crucial to make time each day to be quiet and be in touch with your spirit self."

We understand that the journey of accepting these difficulties and taking steps to be free of them is an opportunity to learn lessons for life.

"When I think about this statement I become quite irritated," admitted Colin.

"The point of the idea, I think, is to reduce the impact of any problem. Our challenges are actually compounded when we think: 'it's me, it's my fault, and I'm always going to be this way'.

Problems are eased if, as Gabby says, we are able to shrug our shoulders, accept the situation and treat our difficulties as opportunities for learning and personal growth.

The statement is not meant to belittle our life traumas, as perhaps your irritable reaction suggests?"

We will be kind to ourselves especially throughout our difficult experiences.

"There's a difference between being kind to yourself and being soft and self-indulgent, isn't there?" suggested Sophie.

"It's definitely a personal thing: to know if it's appropriate to 'pull yourself together' as some might say, or when to sensitively take time to acknowledge, allow and accept."

"I've often heard you use the 'triple A' as you call them, Vanessa. Will you explain what it means to acknowledge, allow and accept?" Frank asked.

"Acknowledge who you are: know that your real self is your spirit.

Allow your choice of behaviour, and that of others, without judgment.

Accept that your choices are the adventure of life."

"Those instructions seem rather passive - as if we shouldn't make any effort - and they imply something similar to fate; it all seems rather irresponsible to me," Colin remarked.

"On the contrary: The first 'A' – to Acknowledge – is a way of actively connecting to your spirit self; and having done so, the remaining two - Allowing and Accepting - naturally follow as wise methods of living; in fact, when the act of remembering your spirit self becomes a natural part of your daily routine, you will be surprised how your life unfolds in a positive and proactive way."

"Why is that?" asked Laura. "Why does it seem that things work out well when we've been paying attention to our spirit self – such as when we meditate?"

"The universe has a natural law: tidal flow, decay and renewal, coming and going... everything works for the greater good, for highest good. During meditation you gift yourself specific moments to flow in perfect synchronicity with everything; this means you become perfectly aligned with the universe, working with the flow, not against it. The experience is what I like to think of as 'universally natural', a way of 'being' as opposed to trying, doing and thinking.

And, by the way, Laura, I'm glad you've taken to meditation."

"So am I. It's helped me through a great deal of pain and difficulty. In fact Frank and our children take 'time out' regularly; we've discovered that just a few minutes improves the day."

We have the wisdom not to dwell upon our difficulties, nor speak about them in ways which cause them to be reinforced.

"Laura has been a wonderful ambassador for this one," said Frank. "I'm told that she's been an inspiration for other patients in the cancer ward."

"I remember the first time I heard her speak about cancer," Malcolm remarked, "it brought tears to my eyes. She said: 'I'm not beating this. There is nothing to fight. I am neither at war with my body nor the disease. It will not become the preoccupying topic in my family's life. It is simply a part of my journey which I am learning to embrace, and then move through.'"

"Wow, Malcolm, is that what she said? You remember her exact words?" Frank exclaimed.

"She impressed me so much, I had to remember them."

Whether our difficulties continue or whether we become completely free of them makes no difference to who we are.

234

"We've certainly added to our vocabulary since we've met Vanessa!" said Colin. "We 'be' and we have a 'true self' which is our 'spirit'. We've learned that our spirit is the wise part of us that we uncover when we find stillness during meditation. What else?"

"We've learned to ask 'Who Am I?' whenever we become wrapped up in the difficulties of the material world," added Malcolm, "and we definitely need the next statement on your list:"

We love our self "just as we are."

"Yes," Vanessa confirmed, "when we repeat, 'Who am I?' as a mantra we begin to come to terms with ourselves 'just as we are', because the phrase keeps the mind from settling upon who we are *not*.

Let me explain: Throughout our life we tend to define ourself by the world's criteria; this sometimes creates problems when our chosen identity ceases or when it no longer gives us fulfilment. For example, if our head-teacher defines his reason for 'being' by his position in our school and within the community, he may find life difficult when the time comes for him to retire."

"He'll wonder who he is for a long while," said Colin, sadly.

"Exactly. And so it's wise to use the meditative reminder: 'Who Am I', and to train our mind to realise who we are *not*: not just a head-teacher, not just a parent, not just a human body, not just an attractive person, not just a thoughtful mind, not just a nice person.

235

In fact, deeply spiritual individuals will repeat the mantra without looking for a resolution; they know that they are part of a miraculous universe, and welcome their relationship with the power behind its creation, so the world's labels are inadequate to explain 'Who Am I'. Indeed, ultimately the realisation that we are none of the world's defining essentials brings us to an appreciation of the Infinite."

"Umm," Frank pondered, "When I think about 'Who Am I?' it makes me wonder who, or what, it is that I love in another: it can't be that I love her as her body, because when the body becomes less perfect, I still love her perfection."

"It can't be that I love my family when they're good," Maria joined in, "because I love them when they're definitely not bein' good."

"It can't be that I love just through intimacy," said Sophie's husband, gaining confidence in his new environment, "because even when that fails, I still love and am loved."

"It can't be that I love perfection in others," said Gabby, "because even when I see imperfection in myself and others, I still love."

"How is it possible to love, when everything is taken away?" asked Colin, close to tears.

Frank's daughter raised her hand to speak; despite her youth she was accustomed to having her thoughts taken seriously, especially at home whenever she joined in meaningful discussions with her parents, "I've been making sense of this idea by thinking about computer terminology."

A mocking groan from one of her brothers was instantly silenced by a "look" from Maria who still maintained her habit of disciplining both families.

The young lady ignored her brother's teenage embarrassment and stood up to explain her idea: "My whole self is a like a wonderful computer: it has a software program that controls my body, one that drives my feelings and another that switches into my thoughts; I choose and click upon different applications for living. But there's a special program that constantly runs in the background unnoticed by the rest of my software: it is the program of my spirit self. And I've made the important decision to have this background program as my 'default' so that my life is controlled by my spirit, then I am always happy with Who I am."

Her audience applauded while Frank and Laura, seated across the room, beamed with pride at their daughter's poise and originality.

"We've all been working on unusual ideas," she continued, "you've written a fun story haven't you?" she said, glancing towards her friend, Malcolm's daughter.

"I think you should read that story," said Vanessa, "but wait until we're all completely settled before you begin."

Malcolm looked quizzically at his daughter, though his expression turned somewhat fearful as he glanced towards the door.

"Who is that?" whispered Gabby.

"The striking lady who's just arrived? Guess," said Sophie.

"It's not...his wife?"

"Oh yes. Attractive isn't she?"

"Surely he's not left her for... no wonder he's been in such a state. Why has she turned up, do you think?"

"I think she's come to see the result of Frank's work with the youth group. A while ago he asked my husband and my sister-in-law to help because the meetings are turning out to be quite the place to be if you're about sixteen! The kids are keen to take part in the group's activities; I don't think low self-esteem is their problem," Sophie laughed.

Malcolm's daughter looked directly at her audience; she had inherited her mother's attractive appearance and her father's communicating charm:

"Hello everyone. Our youth group has been on a mega shopping trip together, organised by Frank," she scanned the room and smiled at him. "We came across a dough-nut bar where, not only could we buy a boxful...each, but we were also able to watch them being made. I thought it was really cool, because Vanessa talks about a doughnut in our centre which needs to be filled with inner light instead of jam."

Her audience chuckled.

238

"Anyway. I thought about a young doughnut who couldn't figure out what was happening in his life, and this is his story:

Dough felt really happy and excited that he had been created, especially in the 'Krispy Kreme' kitchen; he was sure his life would be a dream of soft, spongy togetherness.

Then a separating knife came along and isolated him from the mass of one mixture; he felt sad and alone.

He was massaged and moulded into a perfect ring with an immaculate centred hole. He was proud of his shape and his independence: now he was made, life would be good.

Turning 'round' he realised he was en route to an enormous bath of hot oil, 'Help, help,' he screamed, 'I'm going to be burned and greasy.'

He took a deep breath as he was guided into the tank. But being cooked gave him firm structure and a lovely golden colour; no longer did he feel pale, wobbly and vulnerable in the outer world. His oily hot dunk was a blessing.

Shaking himself with strength and vigour he began to breathe with eager anticipation when suddenly he was showered with plumes of sugar; coughing and spluttering he thought his shiny body was spoiled, but catching sight of himself in the shiny stainless steel machinery, he saw the effect of his coat, and felt sweet. Perhaps he would find love.

Encased in glass for all to see, he knew he'd made the right life decision; from here people would admire him and he could see the world – at least the path outside and part of the shopping centre...

After a while, with nothing happening, he felt bored and disappointed; perhaps he'd made the wrong life choice after all? Then suddenly lights blazed around him, the day was turning into a busy one with noise and excitement, he shifted his icing with anticipation.

Sadly other doughnuts were being lifted away from him into firm cardboard boxes with eleven other friends. Surely he ought to be one of the party? He longed to be chosen. To remain would be to grow stale and eventually be thrown into a rubbish bin, and he'd heard stories of discarded doughnuts tossed with their coffee cups onto the grass verge to be pecked by passing crows. He shuddered at the thought...

Then, suddenly, what bliss and joy, he heard that he had been chosen, and he was carefully lifted off his shelf and placed in a box. This was his plan, his ultimate life goal – to be boxed and purchased.

But the box was not how he'd hoped; the cardboard became soggy as his greasy bottom stuck to its surface. This was not the plan; perhaps he should have welcomed more sugar? Or bathed for a shorter time? Or made his shape more dense? Or kept himself together? OR NOT BEEN BORN AT ALL?

His musings took less time than he thought. His human was hungry and greedy; he watched with horror as all his friends were stuffed into a very wide mouth. Was this his destiny? If he remained his life would be a slow decline into hardness, mould and ugliness. He knew he must go on, be bitten, swallowed and digested...Though it didn't seem so bad as he became integrated into the world of Oneness...

So, if you think your life at the moment feels like a whirl of indecision in a world of poor decisions; make a new decision:
Become a 'Dunkin' Donut'!

You may not understand the point of my story, so I'd like to help you get my meaning by saying something important – in front of you all; in fact, something very important to my Father:

Dad, even though we've been having a tough time at home, I do love you. I love you so very much..."

Malcolm stumbled across the room, his daughter rushed towards him, and as they came together she snuggled her body against his in a daughter's loving embrace.

Chapter 18   Illumined Darkness

"I'm sure I have you to thank for my daughter's change of heart," said Malcolm, shaking Frank's hand. "Her Mother tells me that at home her typical response in most conversations requiring an opinion is: 'Frank says...'!

You know, you've done a wonderful job with our youngsters, and I am particularly grateful for the support you have given her... especially at this time when she's in need of someone she knows she can trust."

"She is a well-balanced young lady; you and your wife must be very proud of her. By the way, how are things between you?"

"We're working through our divorce with as much good will as possible, but it's not easy; it hurts to see the devastation I've caused."

"Yes; and it hurts me too," Colin interrupted, "when I see two innocent wives suffering: yours and Frank's. I know how painful it is to watch a wife suffer; for sixty years my wife and I were together, sixty years meant something, and I made sure I did what I could to ease her pain... What you're doing is not right, it's just not right."

"Colin, Colin, you're tired; you've had a strenuous evening in front of a large audience; let me walk you home so you can get an early night," said Frank.

"No, no; not just yet: the children, their parents and our invited guests are gradually leaving, and the rest of our evening agenda is set; Vanessa has yet to speak to our small group, and I'm keen to hear her, though I'm not sure what she might say; I hope she isn't going to start talking about God, I really can't face the idea of her preaching to me."

Malcolm and Frank exchanged glances: Colin's belligerent behaviour concerned them, and his shadowy grey pallor suggested that he was tired and somewhat overwhelmed by the evening's exertion, so Malcolm tried his own approach to pacify the old man: "We're all excited about our blossoming community, and sometimes our emotions make us say things without thinking, Colin; and really, you know one thing for sure: Vanessa has never, ever preached to us."

"Yes, yes, that's true; I'm sorry, I hope she didn't hear me; indeed, I hope she doesn't concentrate her thought on me, I really couldn't bear it."

"You're just a little disappointed, Colin," Malcolm grinned.

"You should talk," the old man responded, bitterly.

Frank frowned and shook his head, he was perturbed at the old man's comments, and as he firmly guided him to his seat he continued his soothing words: "Look, Vanessa is ready, let's calm down and listen to her."

Vanessa waited until they were all settled, but instead of sitting as part of the group she walked around the circle of chairs so that she could interact with each of them individually.

She hugged Sophie, placed her hand near her tummy, and then her heart; she took the young woman's hand and placed it in her husband's grasp. Seated side by side, they smiled at each other as Vanessa's palm hovered over them, as if in blessing.

She moved to Gabby, placed her hand on the woman's head and heart, and whispered, "Dear, Gabby; let go, let God. Let go, let God." Gabby nodded as a single tear rolled down her cheek.

Maria received a long hug before Vanessa took her protégée's hand and guided it to touch both their hearts. The younger woman copied the movement, touching Vanessa's heart, and then her own.

Frank allowed Vanessa to draw his head to her heart, and in an attempt to prolong the moment he wrapped his arms around her; then he released his hold and looked searchingly into her eyes.

Laura and Vanessa embraced as firm friends, "Life is good," the healed woman murmured, "thank you, Vanessa; life is very good."

Malcolm and Colin reacted in very different ways to Vanessa's approach: Malcolm, now comfortable with his customary greeting, took hold of her hand and whispered, "Vanessa, I love you. I love you so much."

But Colin resisted her embrace, "Don't touch, please don't touch me; I can't bear it." Vanessa allowed her hand to linger over Colin's head, and then she returned to her seat.

"My dear friends, this evening has been a blessing for us all, and I'd like to continue to talk about the statements that we have come to know as our 'Lore.' We did not mention earlier all the phrases that make up Colin's list, but now I would like to speak about the final one. It is this:

We see the light of the inner spirit of everyone; it is Love.

Let's ask ourselves again: What is it about others that we love? Their body? The loving behaviour of the body? Or something we perceive inside and around it?

Over the past few months you have all been intent upon an accelerated soul journey: you've learned to acknowledge the presence of your spirit, and understood how it ought to receive your attention.

As you continue your adventure, you will see the light of the inner spirit of everyone in spite of everything else that they present to you:

When your eyes see a sick body, your heart will see the light shining forth, and you will know that the person is whole.

When your emotions sense other people's anger, fear, hatred and self-loathing, you will feel warmth flowing through your second chakra, and you will know that as a result of your presence, their emotions will find balance in the rediscovery of peace, love and self-esteem.

When your mind finds confusion, betrayal, dismay and powerlessness, you will experience the light at your solar plexus which confirms reliability and limitless power at the centre of your being.

When your spirit is daunted by a world that does not remember itself, the light from above will enter your crown, find itself in your heart, and shine strong as a beacon of Pure Love.

You will know all these things, naturally; you will grow in wisdom and find fulfilment and purpose, not through your actions, simply through being. And whenever you see Light in another you will know it to be a reflection of yourself."

They sat in awed silence. Vanessa's words were not consciously understood, but they were aimed at their hearts; and together they knew she had successfully found her target.

"May I ask a question?" said Sophie, tentatively.

"Of course, I wish you would: whenever we've been together – here at Sputnik's Hub or in my home - we've always found that discussion helps us all towards a clearer understanding of life's mystery, and your questions and comments help me to know what more I must say, and when I ought to keep quiet!"

"Well... I wanted to know... When you speak of the light from above, do you mean God? I've been wondering ever since I saw some sort of light through Laura when we met in your home, and I'm still not sure what it was; I can hardly believe I saw God."

"You mustn't talk about seeing God," interrupted Gabby, "it makes me feel uncomfortable."

"Me too," Colin murmured, "I'm not ready to see my Maker, and He certainly won't want me in heaven."

"This is where our discussion stumbles through misunderstanding and transpersonal difficulties," Vanessa

246

replied. "In fact, I've heard it said that our thoughts about God tell us more about our perception of self rather than any understanding of the Divine."

"You mean, I'm afraid of talking about God, because I am fearful of Him," said Gabby.

"And fear often brings up anger," said Vanessa, glancing at Colin.

"So you're not afraid of God?" queried Gabby.

"Not even in awe?" asked Sophie.

"It's perfectly fine to have multiple feelings about our relationship with the Divine," said Vanessa quietly. "Sometimes we want to be nurtured, safely enfolded in the heart of God; at other times, with a change of emotion – perhaps in fear – we want to be totally forgiven; then there are instants when the human mind wants to understand the creative power of an eternal force; and in finer moments, we seek ways to praise and adore the Infinite and Unknowable.

There are those for whom God is an Almighty power: distant, eternal, creative and protective; to them, God is transcendent; for others, God is an everlasting Presence perceived within; to them, God is immanent; and for a few, God is both transcendent and immanent; to them, God is The All and is totally expressed by all."

"How does 'Who am I?' help our understanding of God?" asked Malcolm.

"When you allow yourself to meditatively flow with that question, and have the question flow through you, you'll find yourself letting go of your identity as a physical body, an owner of material things, a personality, or a certain person in society; and as these concepts are relinquished you embrace the realisation that you are a perfect expression of God. Paradoxically, when this revelation occurs, all the worldly labels you momentarily discarded become part of you again, and subsequently you see them – and you see yourself with them - in a completely different light: the light that is God."

"Are you saying we are God?" asked Frank, "because I find that difficult to accept."

"A mystic is happy to say, 'my me is God', and he will also affirm that this is true for everyone."

"And what would *you* say? How do you feel about God?" asked Maria.

"I'm in love with God," said Vanessa, softly, "and... I can't help it."

"Stuff and nonsense," blustered Colin, "your comments go too far for me, Vanessa. I can't take any more of this." He struggled out of his chair and with difficulty paced around the room. "Really...I can't take any more... all this talk is blasphemous; what will God do to me when He knows I've been listening to this? How am I going to face Him? What am I to do?...

...This evening I heard you, Malcolm, talking about how you've hurt your wife...

...And then there's your wife, Frank, she's hurting too...

...It's not right... and I just can't take any more...

...She haunts me, you know, haunts me."

"Who, Colin?" asked Maria, gently. "Who is haunting you? Your wife?"

"No, no; HER..." he cried, pointing at Vanessa.

"Now Colin, calm down; we told you a while ago you're probably over-tired," said Frank. "Come, I'll walk home with you. You'll feel better in the morning."

"No, no, no... I won't feel better...ever. Though..." he added, with sudden calmness, "there is one thing that you can do for me, Frank."

"What Colin? You know I'll do anything I can to help you."

"Please, will you take my dog and let him be with your children? He was so playful when they fussed over him. They'll look after him for me, won't they?"

"Why, Colin?" Laura asked, searchingly. "You and your dog are so happy together. Why do you want him to be with the children?"

"Because tomorrow... Tomorrow, I have to give myself up. She's tormented me enough. I have to turn myself in."

"What do you mean?" asked Frank, urgently.

"Don't you see? *She* sees, I know she does. She's seen right through me from the beginning."

"What has Vanessa seen?"

"She knows that it was me who put an end to the suffering. I stopped it. Early one morning the sun shone through our bedroom window, the birds were singing... it was a brand new day, and I couldn't stand it anymore. I had to put a stop to her suffering...she put her hand out and the

dog came to her, she touched his head and sort of relaxed...
so then I knew she was dead. It was me. I killed her." He
looked directly at Vanessa, "I killed my wife."

There was prolonged silence; nobody moved; their
breath seemed to hang in the heavy atmosphere of the room.

"Well...it can't be...murder," said Gabby, slowly and
quietly.

"She was near to death," added Sophie, "everyone in
the village knew how well you cared for her, for months and
months."

"Years. I cared for her for years. At first it was like
taking a small child out for a walk, holding her hand
wherever she went, even throughout the house. I quite liked
that; it felt tender. Then gradually she lost sight of me, you
know?" He started to cry. "She'd look at me so vague and
uncomprehending so that my heart hurt. After a while I'd
find her doing such strange things: can you imagine how
many unusual places a woman thinks she should go to the
toilet? I'd get angry and she'd look at me with vacant
soulful, yet soul-less eyes.

Finally, it became easier when she could no longer
move; at least then I knew I wouldn't lose her. But I did lose
her; when she looked at me, where was she? Where did she
go? For months towards the end I fed her using a child's cup
with a spout... she had a bib...and a nappy...I couldn't stand
it...couldn't face any more days and months...

And then there's the problem of the money."

"Money?" Malcolm queried. "I've occasionally joked with you about the extent of your pension."

"Pension...and insurance..."

"Oh."

"What would you like us to do for you?" asked Vanessa, as she moved to stand close beside him.

"I'd like Frank to take my dog to his children; they will love him. Then I'd like you to pray for me because tomorrow I'm going to 'turn myself in' as they say."

"Please don't do that," wailed Gabby, "none of us will say anything; your wife was close to death, in fact you've described how she hadn't really been living for a very long time. You stopped her suffering because you loved her...you still love her."

"It haunts me, she haunts me," he murmured. "I must go to the police, and I will. Tomorrow."

"And I'll come with yer," said Maria, firmly. "I've had experience of that place with the kids...it's not nice. You'll need me by yer side."

"Thank you," he smiled, "now, if you don't mind, I'll go home now."

With heavy hearts Frank and Malcolm accompanied the old man to his house; they continued to be concerned at his appearance and at the sudden apparent decline of his energy; for the first time in their friendship his frailty matched his age, but despite their urgent pleas he refused to have them keep him company through the night.

Chapter 19   Home-coming

Maria and Frank arrived at Colin's home very early the following morning. Colin had insisted that only Maria should accompany him to the police station, but later, Frank had persuaded Maria that he should also be there to support her.

The curtains were still closed, but this was what Maria expected; she had become accustomed to calling on Colin quite early to help with cleaning and to ensure that his refrigerator was adequately stocked: of late the old man had relied on meals at Sputnik's Hub and had lost the habit of shopping even for breakfast and supper requisites.

Maria opened the door carefully, expecting to be greeted by the dog; she had forgotten that he had already been welcomed into his temporary home with Frank's children.

She called her familiar greeting, "Where are yer?"

Frank glanced questioningly at her.

"It's ok, he's usually in bed, and he's sumtimes a bit deaf at this time of day; by the time I've worked my way through the rooms doin' the curtains he'll be amblin' around," she grinned. "Colin! Frank's here too; hope yer don't mind!"

"He's got himself prepared," commented Frank, "look here, poor man, he's packed what looks like an overnight bag. Do you really think they'll detain him?"

"No tellin'," she murmured, "depends what mood they're in."

"No, really? You're kidding, right?"

"Remember, I've done a few of these trips, usually with a sullen teenager, and once with my 'usband."

"You *are* kidding!"

"I'm not," she retorted grimly.

"Oh, Maria!"

"He was *innocent*... really. Yer didn't think my 'ubby... oh Frank, I 'ave some very unruly kids, but we're not bad, yer know."

"I know, I'm sorry; and Colin isn't 'bad' either. I hope he'll be helped by a good lawyer... But, where is he?"

They went into the bedroom and found him, silent and peaceful, in bed.

"Oh my God," she screamed, "oh no, oh no...he hasn't...has he?"

"His body is quite cold, so he's been dead most of the night I should think," said Frank assuming his professional role. "It looks to me as though he died in his sleep, though obviously the doctor, police and a coroner's officer will confirm this."

"Hell," she gasped, "there's his pen and paper by the bed."

Frank glanced over the spidery writing. "I'll not touch anything, but to set your mind at rest, this is just figures, perhaps setting his finances in order; honestly, there's no self-incriminating note here."

"Thank God," she breathed.

"We'll leave these curtains, and I'll make the necessary phone calls...

Did you hear someone at the door?...

Oh...Vanessa," he exclaimed, "why am I not surprised to see you?"

"I thought I might be needed," she said. "Is everything in order?"

"Completely in order," Frank responded.

"He's gone," added Maria.

"Home?"

"Yes"

"Ah, he did say so," she murmured to herself.

"He said so?" queried Frank.

"Last night...his final words to the group...didn't you hear?..." Vanessa clarified her thought: "...His parting request: 'if you don't mind I'll go home now.' ...So I assumed this would be his decision."

"*His* decision?" Frank exclaimed. "You're suggesting he knew he was about to die?"

"A part of him knew, I'm sure," said Vanessa. "His soul's timing was wonderful, don't you think? Now, do we have time to offer some sort of closure on his behalf before the officials arrive?"

"He did ask us to pray for him," whispered Maria.

"And so we will."

Vanessa stood at the end of the bed while Maria and Frank moved to be on either side so that Colin's body was surrounded by loving presence. Vanessa held out her arms in open supplication, "Dear Colin, you are surrounded by unconditional love and absolute forgiveness; go safely into the Light, dear friend, with our love."

"Amen."

"And now, with power from our heart we affirm that this house is cleansed and cleared of all lingering unhappy energy, and we request that the spirit which we know as Colin, and that of his dear wife, are safely and completely guided to The Light, to God - returning home, as he said.

And so it is."

"So it is," Maria echoed.

Many people attended Colin's funeral; he had gained the affection of the community during his daily walks, and his presence in the village was greatly missed.

After the ceremony Vanessa invited the "Sputniks" to her home; the group now included Sophie's husband who had become another enthusiastic member, and also, on this occasion Maria's husband joined them, recognising the need to be close to his wife as she managed her grief.

The friends' sense of loss was tinged with relief that Colin's distress was over; for them his passing brought his challenging situation to a satisfactory conclusion.

As they began to relax in the peace-filled environment of Vanessa's home, they learned that Colin's bedside writing was a financial instruction for monies to be redirected from his estate to his insurance provider in respect of his wife's life policy. Although the news was pleasing, it brought some concern that his action would be seen as an admission of wrongdoing. In any event, Malcolm and other officials who had oversight of the community's funds were assured that Colin's generous donations were actually gifted from his personal account; and so the group's warm memories of the old man - his companionship, presence and generosity - remained unspoiled.

"We should name sumthin' after him," said Maria, tearfully.

"I've been thinking about that," Malcolm replied. "Whenever I think of Colin I recall his natural love for children, not only as an interested retired head-teacher, but also as a man who sincerely wanted the best for every child in our community. There was one occasion when he positively lit up with enthusiasm when talking with Stevie about his future."

"I remember that as if it was yesterday," said Maria, brightening. "It might 'ave bin the start of our Stevie's career."

"Indeed. That's why the school governors have a plan to set up a trust in Colin's name to encourage and help children just like Stevie."

"That is truly wonderful," Gabby exclaimed, "and I for one will be delighted to contribute something annually."

"That's most generous and thoughtful, Gabby, thank you," Malcolm responded, "and maybe in the future there will be contributions from the Sputnik organisation which will permanently keep the remembrance of Colin in the community and within the group."

"Great idea," said Frank, "and we should create a committee to ensure that donations and support are thoughtfully directed."

"Another committee," muttered Maria.

"They're right, yer know," her husband replied.

"Well, you join the committee then, if yer think it's such a good idea!" she retorted.

"I will!"

"And you're very welcome!" Malcolm's rapid response was accompanied by laughter at Maria's wide-eyed astonishment.

Vanessa moved around the room serving their tea like a doting mother, "Tell us about Colin's other writing that night, Frank."

"Oh yes! At the end of the list of figures, Colin finished the page with two statements from Sputnik's Lore:

We recognise that the challenging behaviour of others may be the result of their difficulties of self-acceptance.

We see the light of the inner spirit of everyone; it is Love."

"It's truly wonderful that his last hours were fixed upon self-forgiveness and enlightenment," said Vanessa. "We should be glad that, without doubt, his passing would have been peaceful after having written those words, and we should feel honoured that because of our Sputnik gatherings he spent time composing his thoughts to give us our 'Lore'; he had the tenacity to present his statements to us, and finally left us with guidelines for life; indeed, we've been gifted with wisdom for living."

"It's a wonderful legacy," murmured Sophie.

"It was his plan," Vanessa replied. "The day he and I met he said he wished to be of use to the community."

"He certainly was," Malcolm murmured.

"And will continue to be," added Gabby.

They sat in silence for a while, in deep reflection.

Frank interrupted their stillness: "Vanessa, as usual your comments keep nudging my curiosity, and I've been wondering about something you said when you joined Maria and I at Colin's bedside…about Colin making the decision to die that night… And I've noticed how you seem to have an uncanny ability to recall people's comments… and then you have a habit of suggesting a connection between their conversation and subsequent events; it all seems rather mysterious; please will you explain?"

"She's gonna say: it's all about, Who Am I," Maria grinned.

"Yes, that may be the short answer to most metaphysical queries!" laughed Vanessa. "However, let me draw your attention to one of our Sputnik's Lore statements – the one that says:

We understand that the journey of life is an adventure of the heart and soul.

Think of it like this: our spirit or soul wants the best for us, and it is satisfied when life's adventures lead us to an understanding of 'who we are.'

When we set aside time for stillness through the practice of meditation we give precedence to our spirit, and this leads us to make life choices which are in synchronicity with the bigger picture of the universe; meditation does not make us different, but it does bring a sense of awareness of our highest good, and sometimes significant words slip from our lips which are an indication that we are consciously aware of our own grand plan."

"So it wasn't fate that caused Colin to die just before he was about to turn 'imself in?" Maria queried.

"Colin's spirit self knew he'd reached a stage where he'd learned enough for this lifetime, and that particular night's choice presented an opportune moment for his spirit to leave his body."

"Death frightens me," said Gabby. "When I heard that Colin had gone, I looked out of my window into the dark night and thought of him alone in the cold; I felt terrible."

"Death upsets me because it's the end of everything; my babies were given a life, but it was taken from them forever; they never had a chance," murmured Sophie, bitterly.

"You don't think like that, do you Vanessa?" said Malcolm, warmly. "Tell us your thoughts."

"I know the truth of reincarnation," she said firmly. "Our personal spirit is an aspect of the cosmos which lives on and on from one lifetime to another. When our body is conceived our spirit takes its place in and around us; it animates the body, and it is the cause and reason for life in a body.

Actually, when we use 'Who Am I' as a repeated meditative mantra, we realise that our spirit self is our real 'me' which carries a particular agenda for our life adventure."

"So, as we die, our spirit leaves?"

"It's a soul decision."

"Really? So our death isn't because of fate, or God, or just bad luck."

"Undoubtedly there are choices right up to the point of our spirit's departure. If it were not so, we would just be predetermined puppets, and there is little point in that," Vanessa remarked.

"I'm rather troubled about the idea of a personal choice for my moment of death: somehow it makes it seem even more scary because it implies that I will have to make that important decision; how will I know when the time is right? And how can you be sure that this is what actually happens?" Gabby asked, irritably.

"Whether as a result of an accident, a slow decline, or an untimely early departure, our *spirit* takes the decision to leave the body, and at the same time the body relinquishes life force," Vanessa explained, gently. "We each exist as three components: our spirit, our body, and an energy which animates the body. To explain how these work together we should think of the example of a flower: just as the life-giving nutrient of the flower returns to its bulb, so the body's life energy returns to the 'ether'; and just as a leaf, stalk and bloom of a flower wither, so our body withers and dissipates into earth. Meanwhile our spirit, with all its significant memories of life's learning, departs to exist in the world of consciousness, awaiting its decision to begin another life in another body."

"I wish I could believe this," whispered Sophie, "it would make me feel happier if I knew that my first two children were not totally gone."

"Well, in my job I've heard many strange stories of people who declare they had premonitions about their accident or incident," remarked Frank. "And actually, one of my colleagues, who died quite suddenly, left his office and desk uncharacteristically tidy; the team commented at the time that it seemed as though he'd cleared up before he departed!"

"Our discussion makes death seem much less frightening," said Laura. "For me, I feel confident that my natural self is in charge; my end will be a planned inner agreement between my personal me and my spirit me; I will not be forever floating in the dark and cold, and I will not disappear forever."

"Well said!" Vanessa exclaimed. "And you, my dear, are not leaving for a *very* long time."

"I know," she said, glancing lovingly towards Frank.

Vanessa was keenly aware that their discussion had become extremely intense and difficult, and so she suggested that they should continue to relax in her home and garden while she prepared further refreshment, "When you've had time to reflect I have something more I'd like to tell you," she announced, seriously.

Malcolm joined her to help prepare their food, "Do you think they'll find all this rather too surreal? Will they be able to accept your explanations, do you think?"

"It is challenging for most adults who have grown up with a fear of death, and even more difficult when some have accepted mysterious ideas about the whole life process - such as the debate about fate, or the notion of an existence with no personal reason for life's adventure; however, I trust that gradually their interaction with their spirit self will bring enlightenment.

You know me, Malcolm; you're aware that I wouldn't want them just to accept what I have to say, I'd much rather they realised truth as it is personally revealed to each of them, from within."

"But, are you going to tell them?"

"About my personal experience? Yes. I think they're ready, don't you?"

Malcolm put his arm around Vanessa's shoulder, "I have to keep saying: I love you! And I really wish you'd be with us more often - really become one of us."

"You know that's not my way, Malcolm. I have to be alone to do what I do."

"Umm. I know. And I hope you will be able to tell them more about 'what you do.'"

"Let's not get carried away, just carry the food!" she grinned.

After they had eaten, Frank continued his questioning: "Vanessa, Maria and I were glad to have you there when we discovered Colin, and I think we were privileged to experience something special that morning. Please will you tell us what you perceived?"

"It is my belief that Colin went home that night with a conscious intention of preparing himself for arrest the next morning."

"Indeed, Maria and I found his night bag already packed."

"Oh, I don't want to hear any of this," Gabby wailed, "he must have suffered on his own."

"I doubt that," said Vanessa firmly. "That night Colin was fully in touch with his spirit self, knowing that his plans were unfolding for his highest good. Frank and Maria found him lying peacefully in bed with his pen and paper by his side; it is clear that he spent his final few minutes or hours settling the financial issue that had troubled him; and his final written words were of beauty and wisdom which we have already discussed."

"He was ready and prepared for me to go with him," said Maria.

"He was. But then his conscious self and his spirit came to an agreement that the time was right for spirit to leave, for the life force to slowly leave his body, and for the physical self that we remember to begin its decay."

"Your description sounds so cold and mechanical," whispered Sophie, "I'm really quite shocked."

"I'm sorry to be the cause of your shock, dear Sophie," murmured Vanessa. "Actually, the momentous event would have been exquisitely beautiful for Colin."

"How so?" asked Sophie's husband.

"It is highly likely that Colin would have seen beings of light surrounding him."

"Angels?" Maria asked.

"Yes."

"I've seen them."

"You've *seen* angels, Maria?" said Malcolm. "Where? How? When?"

"Wait till Vanessa's finished."

Vanessa smiled. "It's also likely that Colin would have experienced the presence of his wife who would have given him reassurance, enriched his feeling of love and conveyed a sense of bliss. In this state, Colin will have experienced moving towards a bright light, and that will have been the moment that he 'passed'.

Had we been present at his moment of passing we may have heard him cough or sigh; had he been awake we would have been gifted with his blissful expression. However, many people choose not to have an audience when they depart."

"I've heard such stories," added Malcolm, "where a family wait in vigil, anticipating their loved one's passing, and when the mourners take a moment's break and leave the bedside, their loved one dies. Fascinating! Now, may we hear about Maria's angels?"

"They don't look like church ones. They're like movin', floatin' curtains of colour; they flicker around my eyes when I'm doin' sumthin' like the work with Colin's dog, or when I'm thinkin' about what yer need to eat at Sputnik lunches. When I *try* to look for them they disappear, but when I'm just fallin' asleep they are around me. I talk to them and thank them for bringin' us all together."

"Aw, Maria, you are wonderful," Frank hugged her. "Tell us, did you see anything like that when you and I were with Vanessa at Colin's house that morning?"

"No, nothin'. I wish I had."

"Perhaps your shock and distress got in the way of your natural self," explained Vanessa. "And Frank, you wanted an explanation of what happened there?"

"You said a prayer didn't you?"

"Sort of. Let me ask you, as a fire-fighter, when you have attended serious accidents and incidents, are there times when you feel unnaturally uncomfortable after the debris has been cleared?"

"Absolutely he does!" interrupted Laura. "Sometimes he comes home and, even though he's had a shower at work, he strips off his clothes and scrubs himself almost raw in the shower."

"Yes, and there are times when I need to get out in the fields around home and run with our dogs. But I thought this was because of the pungent smell of smoke, and the lingering memory of some of the sights," he added.

"That may well be the case; though the way I see it, a place needs to be cleansed and cleared not only materially by the emergency services, but also in a metaphysical way."

"What does that mean?" Maria asked.

"Well, going back to our scene at Colin's: his home had been filled with the distress of his wife's illness over many years; there was stifling sorrow of their combined suffering, the incident of her death and his subsequent torment.   All of these emotions and events have an unpleasant energy which tends to linger."

"Colin began to talk of feeling haunted."

"He wasn't haunted by his wife, nor by me, though he was beginning to fear the latter; in fact he was surrounded by a pall of unhealthy energy. So, while the three of us were waiting there, I asked for his home to be cleansed of all that unhappiness, and requested that he should be guided to the light."

"Why did you need to request that?" asked Gabby.

"Well, sometimes when the incident of death is sudden, such as a horrific accident, or when there is huge fear of 'meeting the Maker', the person may feel reluctant to greet the light and as a result, they linger around."

"Ghostlike."

"So it needs someone like me to be aware of their hesitancy and firmly direct them on so that they may continue their journey."

"With no fear of meeting God," said Gabby.

"Absolutely no fear," Vanessa looked directly at her. "You never need to be afraid."

"So," said Malcolm taking a deep breath, "tell us how you know this, how is it that you speak about these things with such confidence and certainty?"

"I'll tell you," she said, "after we have had another break."

Chapter 20   Seamless

The afternoon sun helped to lift their mood, and through the cottage windows they could see a patchwork of fields bordered by neat hedges under an expanse of cloudless sky; the scene was idyllic and the atmosphere within was of relaxed peace and inner contentment; the group settled with a sense of well-being despite their earlier debate about disquieting topics accompanied by unusual opinions.

They had become accustomed to Vanessa's habit of serving tea in the manner of a maternal country lady followed by an offering of metaphysical wonder and spiritual wisdom delivered with closed eyes and a serene expression; her presence engendered awe, respect and their unfathomable love.

"Now, what did you ask, Malcolm?"

He smiled, knowing that she did not actually need prompting for she was well able to recall most of their conversations. "You were going to tell us how you know with certainty what happens at death," he said.

She closed her eyes, "I've been there…twice: what happened to me is officially known as a 'near-death-experience'.

The first happened years ago when I suffered the loss of my babies; despite medical intervention it finally became clear that I would never have a family.   Actually, just like Sophie, I was blessed with a loving, supportive husband, but as depressive illness took hold I came to the conclusion that the world, and his love, were not enough to ease my grief."

Sophie's lip trembled and she gripped her husband's outstretched hand, "When you helped me, Vanessa, I had no idea that you were working from personal experience; but now I sense your pain, though I do feel very different about my own loss since you worked with us."

Vanessa seemed not to notice Sophie's compassionate interruption. "My suicidal action was almost perfectly carried out so that doctors had to persist for a long time in order to bring me back. Yes," she sighed, "to 'bring back' is the appropriate description: during their emergency work upon my body I observed their actions from above - as if I was floating over their heads; the phenomenon is called an out-of-body experience, and on that occasion, due to the doctors' skill, and because of my soul decision, my spirit returned to my body and it was brought back to life."

"A sceptic might suggest that your experience was imagination, especially as you must have been distraught with grief and sick with depression," said Malcolm, gently.

"True; and as you know, Malcolm, I have often been my greatest critic. In fact, as I gradually recovered, I did my best to dismiss my experience as some kind of hallucination, but I subsequently learned that out-of-body and near-death experiences can be scientifically verified. Nevertheless, despite such external confirmation, it has always been important for me to be sure that everything I talk about comes from my heart as a result of personal discovery."

"Was your recovery complete?" asked Laura.

"My body regained its health, my emotions gradually settled and my mind recovered its balance, but my view of the outer world was transformed. My sensitivity to other people's thoughts and feelings intensified and I became mystified by conversations and behaviours which did not match what I perceived to be in people's hearts: I saw light and love within others even though they spoke of their anxiety and reacted with fear. The disparity around me became exaggerated, and I grew increasingly troubled and confused."

"Is that when you started meditating?" asked Malcolm.

"It was. I discovered that whenever I created moments of proactive stillness during the day, my health and well-being improved; and conversely, when I rejected what I presumed was spiritual practice, my sickness and sadness returned."

"Why did you reject your spirit self?" Maria queried.

Vanessa opened her eyes and stared directly ahead, "Because I wanted to be normal," she whispered.

"We're so glad you're not," Malcolm murmured. "Please go on; tell us what led to your second near-death-experience."

"It had to happen."

"Had to?" interrupted Frank, "But you have talked about personal choice as well as the soul's agenda!"

Once again she leaned back in her chair and closed her eyes. "As I look back I realise that my soul wanted my complete attention: my spirit was on a mission for me to really find myself. However, I attempted to ignore my inner yearning, and after my recovery I resumed my career and suppressed any idea of following my heart; I failed to listen to my inner self, so my spirit allowed me to go through another extreme experience so that I might have a further opportunity to pay attention to my soul's agenda."

"You tried again?" gasped Sophie.

"No, no; the second near-death-experience was the result of a serious accident. On this occasion I felt as though I was jolted from my body, and when the separation occurred I chose not to go through what seemed to be a tunnel towards an extremely bright light, but instead, I turned my attention to what was going on below me: I watched the emergency medics as they worked on my heart, and I saw my body lying awkwardly on a grass verge.

Actually, this second experience of near-death was miraculous for two reasons: firstly, the wonderful paramedics succeeded in restarting my heart, and secondly, I was later able to be part of scientific research into the phenomenon: university professors analysed my account of the accident and declared that my detailed description of events contained information that I could not otherwise have known except by being somehow conscious in a position detached from my body - in fact hovering over the whole grisly scene.

The scientists' serious research and their absence of scepticism, together with my inner certainty of what I saw, confirmed for me that near-death, and out-of-body experiences occur and are verifiable; and so my acceptance of my heart's direction was complete."

"So the act of facing immanent death changes you?" suggested Malcolm.

"I think so. When you've come close to the experience of bliss and can actually recall it - indeed, when you've had a taste of it - and when you've also endured the moment of wanting to leave... but on some plane of consciousness you choose to return, then your life resumes with intense thoughts about worldly things and desires far greater than anything previously experienced."

"You feel as though you want to make the world a better place?" Maria asked.

"More than that," Vanessa mused. "There is a passionate desire to have everyone else know that there is more to life than what is normally apparent and usually accepted."

"Anything else?" asked Malcolm.

"There is a constant recognition and appreciation of how the world works: a particular knowing about nature, creation, mankind and everything that is the cosmos; it's an indescribable wisdom that continuously bubbles under the surface of consciousness: you know you're in touch with it because it guides you to remarkable things though you feel unable to consciously communicate with it...and so your search goes on...looking for the Infinite."

"Does this mean that you discovered what some people call second sight?"

"It feels utterly beyond and more important than psychic perception," she responded, vaguely, "and, you know, at this moment I feel privileged to have your questions and your love because our conversation has helped me to affirm what my life is about, although words fail to explain its complexity."

"So, as you review your experience of near-death," Frank pondered, "you realise it was necessary for you to go through the dramatic process – twice - so that your soul could reveal itself, and so that you would be sure to give it your full attention."

"And because of yer *acceptance* and *acknowledgment*," added Maria, "yer spirit self stays close, hoverin' just below yer mind's skin, and then yer *allow* its wisdom and power to benefit the world."

Vanessa opened her eyes and smiled; she clasped her palms together and bowed her head in prayerful acceptance: "Thank you, thank you," she whispered. "Your words of wisdom affirm my life's purpose."

There was a communal sigh as if in relief and recognition that something profound had moved the heart of their leader; the group was used to the seamless way she moved between sociable warmth, dry humour, conversational intensity and spiritual depth, but this new situation made them more attentive; after a few moments of fidgeting they gradually followed Vanessa into deep meditative calm; her measured breathing and unmoving eyelids might have suggested to the uninitiated that she was deeply asleep except that her eyes were only partially closed.

Despite their contemplative state Malcolm felt the need to interrupt:

"Vanessa, may I speak?"

"Of course." Vanessa's reply sounded rather distant, and yet quite alert.

"We've become accustomed to meditating with you, and for a while now it has felt natural and normal..."

"Yes... even comforting," Gabby murmured. "But this time it feels different: I still feel safe, but sort of unusual; is it because you have...umm...gone farther away from us?"

"I don't feel that," said Frank. "On the contrary, I'm feeling closer to her; in fact as my breathing deepens I'm feeling particularly close to you all."

The meditative rhythm of their breathing continued, but instead of falling silent with focus upon their breath or personal mantra, they continued to comment upon their emerging visions and experiences.

"I don't know about the rest of you," said Malcolm carefully, "but after an initial tingling through my hands and feet, my limbs now feel as though they have left my body; yet surprisingly I feel more complete, and...well, somehow centred in my middle."

"I can hear my breathing, but it doesn't feel as though it's happening through my body," Sophie whispered, "it's just me and breath, nothing else."

The sound of their breathing filled the otherwise stillness of the room.

"I keep tuning in to the chirping of the birds outside," said Gabby, "they seem closer than normal, though their activity doesn't interrupt my focus; I feel as though I am one of them, tweeting to my mate!"

Frank broke the subsequent prolonged silence with a cough, "I don't share those particular experiences," he said huskily, "but I keep seeing such unusual things."

"Tell us," encouraged Laura.

"It's mostly colour…colour in unusual places…"

"Such as?"

"Well, for a while, whenever I've looked at Vanessa, I've seen bright turquoise on her forehead, as if she has a jewel suspended there; and I used to notice red in the pit of Malcolm's stomach, as if he had an angry fire inside, though now I'm struck by how green his chest appears, especially in the area of his heart."

"Yer seein' things like I do!" Maria exclaimed, "Yer know I've bin seein' energy as colour for a while, but I daren't say much about it in case yer thought I was crazy.

Some of yer look lovely and glowin', 'specially when you've bin meditatin'; and Vanessa, well, I don't see the turquoise, but I do see purple around her most of the time.

And, yer know what? When I'm out and about I see bits of black in some people – around their heart or in their belly – and sumtimes the black goes away if I send pink to them... yer know... like we did ages ago when we sent love from our heart to Gabby.

It doesn't work every time and that's when I get sad; Vanessa's 'elped me with this because it didn't seem normal."

"None of this is normal," remarked Frank, "though it seems to be happening naturally through us."

"Umm," murmured Malcolm, "I guess we need to accept that whatever comes naturally to us *is* normal. I remember Vanessa explaining that we did not come together at Sputnik's Hub to discover something new, but that her aim was to help us to remember what everyday living has caused us to forget."

"Well, I must have completely forgotten everything," sighed Laura, "because despite my interest, enthusiasm and consistent efforts to meditate, I haven't experienced anything like some of you have described."

"Me neither," muttered Sophie's husband.

Vanessa's cough brought their attention back to her presence.

"Sorry, Vanessa," Malcolm frowned, "I didn't realise there was so much to be said; I expect you are used to hearing this kind of bemusement?"

"Actually, over the years I have been used to experiencing it," she said, warily, "so I'm certain that talking and sharing will bring you comfort in the knowledge that you are not alone or abnormal."

"Oh Vanessa, the pain of feeling alone and abnormal hurts me too," Malcolm whispered. "I really am sorry; please will you help us return to the spiritual depth which my conversation interrupted?"

Vanessa smiled fondly at the concerned faces around her and continued to speak in her usual gentle, measured tone, "The image which I have for you will be a special meditation which we should name, 'seamless', because during its process you may well experience a smooth transition between your conscious existence and your boundless self."

She resumed her measured breathing, and with eyes remaining half closed, her soft voice led them deeply within:

"On this occasion we will begin with a focus upon your forehead. First, take deep breaths and imagine how your inhalation rises through your nostrils and fills your head; then listen as you strongly and completely exhale.

Again, deeply inhale... notice the air through your nostrils... your breath fills your head... and strongly and completely exhale...

As you repeat this concentrated breathing, focus your attention inside your head: imagine that you are able to direct your gaze to the inside of your forehead... be patient, don't feel you have to make an effort; let your attention be upon each breath, and focus your gaze on the inside...

It's normally inappropriate for me to make suggestions of what you might perceive, though I can't resist mentioning that at some point during your exploration you may well observe something like a blue sphere amidst the dark inside; whenever that image comes to mind I'm reminded of the 'pale blue dot' picture of Earth...perhaps my consciousness likes to suggest that my meditation takes me far away!

However, forgive me for the digression...let's continue to concentrate upon breathing and allow the focus inside your forehead to be as your subconscious mind wills..."

She paused to allow them time to explore her instructions.

"This is a special 'grounding' procedure," she explained, "but on this occasion we have not started with a focus upon your feet or the base of your spine; instead the exercise enables you to find a foundation at your forehead - your so-called Third Eye; in fact, we could say that this is a way of finding your meditative 'centre'."

The group maintained their attention upon breath and breathing as Vanessa continued her commentary:

"Gradually, your discerning sight may indeed help you to perceive the jewel at the centre of others, and remember - whatever you observe in someone else is actually a reflection of yourself. This centre - at your forehead - is the seat of perception and shines turquoise; it is a beautiful sight, and together with white light your beacon of perceptive love beams upon the world with heightened understanding...

It's likely that many of you will not be able to perceive the images I describe; please don't let this concern you because you can be *certain* that as you look upon others you will see with compassion, and as your gaze rests within, you will probe the Infinite, which, by its very nature, is imperceptible and therefore beyond description."

"So it doesn't matter if I can't see a thing," breathed Laura. "Although actually I feel vacant and vague...and somehow I sense everything..."

"...and nothing," Vanessa helped to complete her observation. "That's beautiful Laura: your experience is stunning... more profound than you realise."

For a while she waited to allow them to continue their breath-work.

"Now, I'd like to continue with images which may help to affirm your connection with each other and confirm your oneness with everything, though in truth this should be expressed as your oneness *as* everything..."

Her students became totally absorbed; their body stilled, they had no inclination to fidget or move for greater comfort.

"...So...whilst retaining your 'grounded centre' through concentration upon breathing into your head... move your attention from the inside of your forehead... to the base of your spine... and visualise red; ...breathe deeply and imagine red bubbling forth from your spine like magma from a volcano... and just as each earthly volcano reaches deep into the centre of the world, so your redness dwells deep within you and spreads from you to merge with the red of others... Indeed, merged together we are an endless sea of red... forever creating and providing life energy.

Imagine that your red naturally 'bleeds' upwards through your spine; it is defining your earthly self, your humus, your humanity; it is a health-giving and life-giving force; it creates and recreates spontaneously, and with love it greets a pool of orange situated just below your navel."

Instinctively the friends reached out to hold hands around their circle, and with continued meditative breathing, they awaited Vanessa's ongoing descriptive image:

"Like an endless sunset, imagine the energy of orange spreading out across your stomach...it spreads out from the sides of your body...and greets the same orange emerging from those sitting beside you; you share emotions and feelings with all mankind, your pain is everyone's pain, and your joys are experienced by all; sunsets and sunrises are one: a collective orange seated and spread across your second chakra.

As you contemplate this connection you may come to realise that the seemingly separate delights and yearnings of mankind are united and experienced in each individual."

Gabby sighed, "Now I know why I so enjoy watching sunsets; I usually wait till the last moment as the sun dips, then I love to see the red and orange cloud spreading across the sky."

The interruption of her soul-full description gave them time to embrace the moment and then they released hands.

"Yes, those evening images are spectacular, and I share your enjoyment," Vanessa replied. "And as we continue, the image of the mid-day sun becomes our meditative focus: just as the sun centres our universe, so we have a sun space in the centre of our self."

She continued to direct their exercise:

"Place your hand on your solar plexus – the space below your heart – and meditatively think of a bright yellow sun... Your brightness is empowering, and as you imagine your breath rising and falling through this place you may feel and use its strength for yourself... so too, your power enlivens and brightens those who you greet with mutual respect. Indeed, your centre of solar energy and brightness are as power and respect shared amongst those who are wise, and with meditative focus each individual creates an evolving world of reciprocity...

Now move your attention to your heart; imagine that your breath rises from your heart and is drawn up through your throat and into your head...

...now imagine the breath returns to your heart to be exhaled from there...

...breath rises from your heart...and is drawn up through your throat...and into your head...then returns to your heart...

Continue this cycle of imaged breathing...

...and now as you image your breath entering your head, imagine that it is retained, swirling inside in shades of blue and purple...

...the colours remain there, energising and empowering, until you choose to send them back through your throat... into your heart... and from there out into the world.

Your heart appreciates this practice because it represents the giving and receiving of energy in an ever constant knowing of itself...

And as this imagery continues you may find that your contemplation leads you to know that your heart is *in* the heart of everyone, and furthermore that your heart *is* the heart of all; and then you will have discovered a significant spiritual truth which will alter your perception of yourself and others forever."

The tone of Vanessa's voice became even softer but gained passion, "I'd like you to intensify your focus upon each breath... watch and listen to your breathing... and gradually allow all the images I have just described to drift away... completely... just focus upon your breath...just your breathing... simply this...your breath... your breathing... and nothing else...nothing... nothing... no thing..."

They remained in meditative stillness for a long time.

Eventually, they each independently finished their meditation and broke away from the circle of seats to seek refreshment and relief, and some wandered into the cottage garden to continue their contemplation.

"Tell me, Vanessa," said Laura, after they had returned to their circle, "why is it that some of us persist in being unable to 'see' the images you describe?"

"There are many ways to access Reality – the powerful Truth that is *within* all of us, and *is* all of us," she replied. "Images and sounds are simply *methods* of finding the way to your deepest self."

"That's why you finished the meditation with just breathin', right?" said Maria.

"And why 'Who Am I' is not a question to be answered," Malcolm commented.

"Indeed. The miracle that is the universe is the self-same wonder that is you, and it is eternally present within you and without; it is truly there - regardless of your perception. In truth, your most profound experience of the Infinite is as nothing, the inexpressible 'no thing' which I mentioned a few moments ago; its depth actually has no words and is beyond understanding."

"Oh yes!" sighed Laura, tearfully, "I sense why you call this experience, 'seamless': spirit within me is imperceptible - it is everything, and yet somehow it is much, much more than the whole of my existence; I have no words to explain what I mean, or describe what I feel..."

"And all we have to do is breathe and focus upon each breath," added Sophie, rather dazed.

"Is it really as simple as that?" Gabby murmured.

"It appears simple because we breathe continuously, but the practice of concentrating just upon our breath and breathing is never easy!" Vanessa smiled.

Then her expression clouded with thoughtful consideration: "Whenever you feel the wonder, or experience the pain of existence, just remember your spirit self; and when people around you appear unresponsive to the wonder of their own infinite truth, simply acknowledge the light that you see within them, and then allow and accept their freedom of choice."

"Even though it 'urts so bad?" said Maria, choking back tears.

"Especially so," she said; and after a reflective pause she continued to express her thought with strength and determination, "Yes! Even when your love for others is unjustifiably painful."

Malcolm left his chair and moved to stand between where Vanessa and Maria were seated; he knelt down, squeezed himself between their chairs and placed his arms across their shoulders; he gently drew them together so that their heads rested against his face; they accepted his hug and held their forehead against his cheeks in a long embrace. "You know," he said solemnly, "you two have put me in touch with my soul and made my heart sing; may your inner joy forever alleviate your outer pain, for you are dearly, dearly loved by us all."

"Indeed, in deed," murmured Frank as he and the rest of the group crowded around the loving huddle.

"We're behaving as though this is a sad departure," said Gabby, "but I know we are actually at the beginning of a remarkable shared journey of self-discovery!"

"Yes! We are! We're Sputniks!" laughed Frank.

Even though they were reluctant to have the meeting end, they eventually made ready to leave, and as they departed they each received an embrace from Vanessa which felt different from hugs they had previously experienced, though none of them spoke about how they felt: they knew that this was one of the moments with her when words were unnecessary.

Slowly they began their stroll back to the village along the riverside path, and frequently they turned to acknowledge Vanessa who watched and waved from her open door.

"She does seem lonely, don't you think?" remarked Gabby.

"I've come to realise that she may be alone, but never lonely," responded Malcolm. "I think Vanessa exists in two worlds: it seems to me that her feet remain precariously poised on the edge of two planes of existence – the material and the spiritual - while her compassionate self bridges the divide."

"And if the two worlds should grow farther apart?" Sophie asked.

"Oh, she'll jump ship, no doubt about that," said Frank, "she's a modern mystic."

He and Malcolm lingered behind the rest of the group.

"Since I've known Vanessa I've frequently and spontaneously told her that I love her; and the more I say it, the more I realise that being around her makes me learn to love myself, despite my inadequacies," said Malcolm.

"I have similar feelings: when I follow her ideas I feel a sort of inner contentment, no matter what's going on around me; and having spent precious time with Vanessa I've learned more about her: I realise how profoundly she loves us and how devoted she is to her work, and that's why I too find it sad that she'll never be part of the group, nor truly accepted or understood by most people.

Have you also noticed how her expression is usually quite serious? In fact when I think about her I'm surprised that she laughs much less than most women," Frank remarked.

"Can't say I've noticed, but when she gets you on her wavelength you discover she has quite a subtle, and sometimes mischievous sense of humour," Malcolm smiled, fondly.

"Yes, I've seen the rapport she creates with everyone, though usually she's quite intense."

"Other worldly."

"Umm."

"Do you know what I heard at the school gate the other day?" Malcolm continued. "Some parents were gossiping about a commotion outside the supermarket a few miles away; they said the row was becoming quite vicious until a woman arrived. Apparently she appeared to glow from her morning walk, and looked as though she'd hiked the fields to get to them. They say that the argument quickly subsided and the group went into the coffee shop together."

"You're kidding!"

"It's what I heard."

"Question is," Frank smiled, "was it inner perception that led her to them, anticipating an opportunity? Or did her spirit self actually *create* it?!"

"Your wife looks incredibly well," said Malcolm, changing the subject.

Frank looked ahead to where Laura's figure silhouetted against the evening sky. "She's beautiful," he breathed, "even though surgeons removed most of her feminine beauty, she's perfect in my eyes...and she still stirs me."

"That's because you love the real Laura," smiled Malcolm. "Do you think Vanessa's work contributed to her cure?"

"Laura declares it is a holistic miracle: medicine, surgery, family love, personal stillness and healing," said Frank.

"Well, I believe in Vanessa's ability to do miracles," said Malcolm, "and when I think about how she works, I hear lyrics in my head from a song written ages ago in the 1960s:

'...you know that you can trust her
For she's touched your perfect body with her mind.'" [1]

---

[1] Leonard Cohen, et. al. *Suzanne,* 1967.

References:

Barlow, G, *Dying Inside*, Sony/ATV Music Publishing Ltd, 2013.

Zeissl, M, Newman, R, Cohen, L, *Suzanne*, Hanseatic Musikverlag, Unichappell Music, Stranger Music, Prophecies Publishing, 1967.

Krispy Kreme Doughnuts, Inc. NC. USA

Dunkin' Donuts, MA. USA

Thank you:

Jacky: for your diligent analysis of the manuscript; your email response was always eagerly anticipated!

Garry: for your creative photography and technical expertise; for listening with an uncanny knowing of what would transpire; and for your companionship and steadfast love on our 'journey'.

Evedon: a beautiful place to enjoy peace and productivity.

Love, Suzanne.

About the author:

After 20 years as a primary school teacher and deputy-head Suzanne's career might have culminated in a position of head-teacher; however, a life-changing battle with illness meant that she discovered her innate ability – to heal self and others, and so her life's purpose was transformed to embrace all that is deeply spiritual.

She spends the greater part of each day in meditation and contemplation, with an inner imperative to understand herself and to know and love God; she is aware that this solitude also benefits others and makes the world a better place.

She offers healing sessions for clients seeking spiritual guidance and has been inspired by those who want to know more about metaphysics: *Sputnik's Lore* offers spiritual teaching in the context of an engaging novel where readers have the opportunity to explore wisdom through empathy with the characters in the story.

'(Suzanne has) the ability to see beyond the apparently incomprehensible and irreconcilable forces of reality into a subconscious – even mystical – parallel world of integrity, meaning and power, which would offer plausible explanations and constructive solutions to present day angst.' R.D.M.

17309567R00162

Printed in Great Britain
by Amazon